TEST #30657
R.L. 4.6
PTS. 5.0

The Cry of the Crow

Also by Jean Craighead George

Julie of the Wolves
winner of the 1973 Newbery Medal

Going to the Sun

The Wounded Wolf

HARPER & ROW, PUBLISHERS

NEW YORK

Cambridge
Hagerstown
Philadelphia
San Francisco

London
Mexico City
São Paulo
Sydney

1817

The Cry of the Crow

a novel by

Jean Craighead George

Library of Congress Cataloging in Publication Data
George, Jean Craighead, date
  The cry of the crow.

  SUMMARY: While caring for a baby crow, Mandy
begins to look at her family and herself in a
different light.
  [1. Crows—Fiction]   I. Title
PZ7.G2933Cr   [Fic]   79–2016
ISBN 0–06–021956–4
ISBN 0–06–021957–2 lib. bdg.

This book is dedicated to

Crowbar, New York, Chicago, Cro-Magnon, Jerry—all the wonderful and unbelievable pet crows I have had or known.

Contents

Prologue

The young crow huddled against her brother in their stick nest in Piney Woods. Her tail feathers were short and stubby; white plumes of down trimmed her head. Her milky-blue eyes were those of an eyas, a nestling bird yet unable to stand on her toes or fly. The pair sat rock still, for their parents were away.

The March dawn was hot and muggy. Insects buzzed around the nest, their glassy wings reflecting the red sunlight. The little female looked past them to a spider spinning her web almost a quarter of a mile away. Her eyes were like telescopes, and she practiced using them while she sat in the nest. Her brother slept, a black lump blending with the black sticks.

Footsteps sounded on the pine needles below and the eyas listened to their beat. *Crunch da dum.* She tensed, for she recognized the footfall of the crow hunter. Her parents had taught her a deep fear of this sound. "Ca! Ca! Ca! Ca!" they would cry at the sound, then pull their feathers against their bodies and crouch silently.

The footfall softened and died away.

Wide-awake now, the eyas heard her parents announce from the Glades that they were on their way home with food. Her ears were as keen as her eyesight. She could distinguish the sounds of her parents' voices from all the other crows of Piney Woods as well as from the clan of crows in Trumpet Hammock, a tree island in the saw grass of the Everglades, a swamplike river that creeps slowly down the tip of Florida under warm subtropical skies.

As her parents flew home, the eyas listened for the voice of the Piney Woods guard crow. He had not warned of the *crunch da dum*, nor did he announce her parents. The forest was ominously quiet and had been ever since the crow hunters began shooting a few days ago.

With a rustle of feathers, her mother alighted on the edge of the nest.

"Ah ah ah, cowkle, cowkle," the eyas begged as she lay on her breast, trembling her wings and opening her beak. Her bill was rimmed with yellow edges. She could not yet eat by herself, for she was only ten days old, and since food had to be thrust in her mouth, the red-and-yellow coloring made it possible for her parents to find the gullet instantly. Her mother stuffed her with delicacies from the Everglades.

Her father arrived, his feathers glistening blue-black in the soft morning light. Her brother begged for food.

From below came a gun blast. Lead balls ripped through

the stick nest. Her father jerked backward, his eyes exploding. Her mother spun around in a burst of feathers. Another blast ripped through her brother and lifted the nest out of the tree crotch. The young eyas gripped a stick as the nest splintered, cracked, then floated apart. She looked down through the pieces and saw the eye and brow of the hunter.

"I got youv," he shouted. The voice and eye were stamped forever on the young crow's mind.

Then she fell.

1
Nina Terrance

Mandy Tressel heard the gun blasts and rolled over in her bed, dragging the pillow down on her ears. She wondered who was shooting at the crows in Piney Woods this morning, her father or one of her big brothers, Jack and Carver. Drummer, her younger brother, was too young to be allowed to handle a gun.

The strawberry crop was coming on and Mandy's father wanted every crow dead before they ate or damaged the valuable fruits.

The odor of gunsmoke trickled through her open window and she got out of bed and looked out. The sun was beginning to light up the strawberry field that stretched from the backyard to the far end of Piney Woods. To the south of their small cinder-block house and the greenhouse, the banana patch grew. The big drooping leaves were motionless in the still air. Even the woman's-tongue tree in the yard, whose seed pods clattered in the slightest breeze, was quiet. The orange and fig trees were still. The buds of the red hibiscus were waiting for the sun before they bloomed. Mandy breathed deeply. The scent of the night-blooming jasmine bush was still on the air although the flowers had closed with the dawn.

Mandy understood why her father wanted the crows killed, but nevertheless she felt sick each time she heard the deafening blasts.

Once, on a family picnic, she had played with a crow in the nearby Everglades National Park of Florida. She was exploring a trail when suddenly the bird alighted beside her and walked with her along the dark mangrove path. She stopped and held out a leaf. The crow jumped nimbly over it, then pecked it. It sat down when she sat down, backed up when she backed up. She realized the bird had come to her for a reason, and leaned down to hear its message. Then Jack called her. The crow listened to his voice.

"Ca! Ca! Ca! Ca!" it cried and stole off between the warped and twisted branches of the mangrove trees. For the entire afternoon she did not see or hear a crow.

The next morning Mandy asked her mother if crows could recognize hunters by their voices. Barbara suspected they did. "They are keen to danger," she said.

As Mandy dressed for school this day, she thought about that mysterious crow and wondered why he had walked with her. Fairy tales of animals who were princes came to mind, but nothing reasonable. She tramped thoughtfully downstairs. Her brothers were already gone; her mother, she could hear, was showering before going to work.

Mandy skipped out the door and ran through the yard to the path beside the strawberry patch that led to Piney Woods. The sun was glittering on the pine needles and she hummed as she swung through a half mile of forest to the golf course in Waterway Village, a cluster of one-story apartments where retired people lived. Barney, the surly dog, barked as she passed Mr. Hathaway's apartment. She stuck out her tongue at him, ran past the swimming pool, and came out on the road where the school bus stopped. The crows and wild things on her mind, she arrived at school in a daydream.

During study hall Mandy wrote a story in her red notebook. She labored hard, erasing and changing the words. Still she was not pleased with what she had written, and coming home through the woods she stopped, reread her work, and changed two more words. A dragonfly spun around her head like a tiny bomber, and a zebra butterfly alighted on her shirt.

"Good omens," she said and hurried on.

As she came to the fork in the path that led to Trumpet Hammock, black feathers from some gunned-down crow swirled up from the ground. She paused and glanced around. Just off the path a sable palm tree grew. It had never been pruned and its old dead leaves hung down like a skirt on a green-headed lollypop. She often came to the palm and crawled between the great drooped leaves. Within this natural tent she read and dreamed in privacy.

Mandy felt as if someone were staring at her. She pushed back a dry palm leaf and peered into the circular room.

Almost at her feet, huddled against a leaf, sat the eyas, gazing up at her. The bird was frightened; her eyes were wide and her feathers were clamped tightly to her body.

"The last nest in Piney Woods," Mandy gasped. "Someone found it, and you're all that's left." She bit her lips together.

The eyas had been studying Mandy in the brief seconds while she peered into the shelter. She had read Mandy's personality through the soft curve of her spine, her curled fingers, and her gray eyes veiled with long lashes. These were readings to be trusted, and she relaxed as Mandy dipped to her knees.

"Oh, poor little bird," Mandy said.

"Ah ah ah, cowkle, cowkle," begged the eyas and fluttered her wings. Opening her mouth, lifting the feathers on her head to make herself round and appealing, she told Mandy very clearly that she was helpless and needed food. Mandy opened her lunch box and took out the crusts of her sandwich.

She held out the food. Once more the eyas fluttered and begged with open mouth. Mandy fed her the remainder of the bread, and when the eyas begged again she wished she had not eaten all of her lunch. Recalling that crows like grubs and worms as well as fruits and grains, she walked into the forest, kicked open a rotted log, and found several beetle grubs. Creeping back under the great skirt of leaves, she fed the bird until she begged no more. Gently Mandy picked her up. The bird had already made her judgment of Mandy. She did not struggle, simply felt the warmth and softness and nestled down in her hands.

"I know you're a girl, so I'll name you Nina Terrance," she said, using the name she would have given herself if she had had a choice. Peering out into the woods to see if anyone was coming, she crawled behind the trunk into her "reading room." The air was cool in the shade of the huge shingles of leaves. Once her father had suggested to her brothers that they rip the old leaves off this sable palm as people do in gardens and along city streets, to make the palms neat and keep them fireproof, but no one had gotten around to it.

"This is your new home," she said to Nina Terrance, standing up in the cool, dark room. Several months ago she had pulled off a few of the inner dead leaves to enlarge the shelter so that she could stretch out and read. Now she had another construction job to do. Placing Nina Terrance on the ground, Mandy skillfully wove the fingers of a drooping leaf into a strong cup, then placed the eyas in it. The bird was about three feet off the ground and secure.

The eyas roused—lifted her feathers and shook them—to say that she was at ease in Mandy's presence and that she liked her. Having been taught by her parents to eat and remain still, she wiggled her stubby tail and sat down in her new nest.

Across the quiet forest came a call: "Ca! Ca! Ca! Ca!"—four sharp reports. The guard crow of Trumpet Hammock was speaking. Nina Terrance pulled in her neck and nestled low in the nest. She had recognized the alarm signal. This was one of about fifty "words" used by the well-organized and highly social crows. This call meant death and danger lurked somewhere nearby.

"What did he say?" Mandy asked the eyas. "Daddy says

crows have a language. He says they can tell each other where the food is or where the enemy is; and that they can warn where death comes from. What did that crow say to make you crouch?"

Mandy dropped to her knees and stuck her head out of the palm tent. No one was coming that she could see, and yet the eyas crow had reacted as if hiding from an enemy.

"Ca! Ca! Ca! Ca!" Mandy hollered, trying to imitate the guard crow. Nina Terrance blinked her eyes as if she had not heard.

"Well, you sure don't know what *I'm* saying." She tried the call again, got no response, and gave up. She stroked the downy head.

"I need practice to pronounce whatever I'm saying in crow talk," she said. "Now don't you move 'til I come." Mandy crawled to the exit and, looking both ways, hurried to find her books on the trail. At the edge of Piney Woods she glanced out across the miles of saw grass that grew in the low water of the Everglades. They plunged and leaped, then Drummer appeared.

"Hey," Mandy exclaimed, happy to see her youngest brother. "Where've you been?"

"Explorin'," he said and Mandy chuckled. Drummer loved the Glades. In this swampy wilderness he pretended he was the great Seminole Indian Chief Osceola, out hunting for his tribe. He threw reed spears at alligators and pounced on frogs.

She glanced back toward the sable palm tree to make certain that Nina Terrance was not following, then walked down the path to the house with Drummer. Mandy swung the gate open and Drummer pushed ahead. Jack and Carver were in the driveway hunched over the engine of their foreign car.

"Hi!" Mandy called to her older brothers. They did not answer, so she walked closer.

"I have something for you," she said.

"I think it's the damn distributor," Jack said to Carver. "We need a new one. Time to put out another issue of *The Waterway Times.*"

"Guess so," answered Carver. "The hardware store is having a sale and Pete wants to advertise by printing coupons to clip. Got any news?"

"No, I don't," said Jack.

"I do," said Mandy.

Jack unkinked his back, stretched, and looked down at his sister. "Another story about a mouse in a closet?" He laughed. "No thanks. We only print news about the *people* in Waterway Village, old people."

"That's just what I've got," said Mandy.

Jack reached into the engine. "Unscrew this bolt and the one under here, Carv," he said. "That'll let the whole thing off. I'll take it to Ray's junkyard. He must have a secondhand distributor. We'll replace the whole thing."

Mandy watched them work for a minute, then turned and walked to the back door. She kicked it open and stepped into the family room, the new addition her father had built last year with the money from the strawberry crop. Three sides of the room were windows. The sun shone in on bookcases, dining table, TV, and chairs. Soft trade winds blew through the room, for the windows were kept open except during storms.

She paused by the bookcase, picked up a copy of *The Waterway Times*, and opened it. The newspaper had been written and typed by Jack, illustrated by Drummer, financed by Carver's selling ads, and duplicated at the Ink Spot, a printing shop in the shopping center on the far side of Waterway Village. She longed to be part of the exciting newspaper that made such a stir in the village whenever it appeared, which was more and more often, for it came out whenever her brothers needed parts for their '59 SAAB. Mandy smiled to herself. Perhaps this time they would accept one of her stories. They needed a distributor and they had no news. She reread the last issue. Stories told of the firing of a nurse at the village, of a great-grandchild visiting; and headlines announced the scores of the golf and shuffleboard contests. Thoughtfully she opened her notebook and reread her own story.

Drummer came in the back door, threw his books on the table, and flipped on the TV.

"Want something to eat?" asked Mandy, closing her notebook. Her voice was so airy that Drummer turned around to see what made her happy this afternoon. He could not guess.

"I'd like a grilled cheese," he answered.

Mandy made two, put one on a plate, and wrapped the other in waxed paper and stuffed it in her lunch box as she called Drummer to eat. Jack came in the door. He was almost six feet tall and seemingly all knuckles and bones. His black hair looked like a motorcyclist's helmet bulging above his wide-spaced blue eyes. Mandy instinctively moved back to make room for this brother whose personality matched his body.

"Well, let's hear your story," he commanded.

Surprised, she knocked over a cane chair as she reached for her notebook.

"Well?" said the editor. "I'm listening."

Mandy cleared her throat. Drummer stopped chewing.

"Bright ripples circled out from the fishing line," she began. "The day was hot and Betty Howard, 73, was hungry. Suddenly her bobber went under. She pulled. A large fish flopped on the end of her line. She reeled in. The fish fought and the water rose in silver fountains.

"After a tiring battle Mrs. Howard landed the fish and pulled it to her feet. For a long time she stared at it. The big sunfish would make such a good meal. The fish gasped in the air and began to die.

" 'You want to live, too, don't you, fish?' she asked; then she stopped, unhooked it, and let it go."

"Aw, come on," said Jack. "Are you kidding? That's no news story."

Carver had come in as she had begun reading and was looking over her shoulder.

"It's not news when a person catches a fish," he said. "Only when a fish catches a person." He laughed at his own cleverness.

"But she let it go instead of eating it," Mandy said. "That's news. Not many people would do that if they were poor and hungry."

"She's nuts," said Jack and picked up the telephone to call the Waterway Village office for news of upcoming trips, games, and visiting relatives.

Mandy closed her notebook, walked through the kitchen, and opened the door to the dark stairs that led to the attic where she and Drummer each had a dormer room. She walked up slowly, head down. Presently the staircase door opened and Drummer climbed to her side.

"I liked your story, Mandy," he said. "I think it *is* news that Mrs. Howard let the fish go. It really is." His brow wrinkled and he ran his fingers through his hair.

"You and Mom don't like wild things to be killed, do you?" he added.

"No."

"What about crows? They eat the crops."

"No."

"But Daddy shoots them."

"Doesn't mean we have to like it."

"Suppose the crows ate *all* the strawberries, then would you shoot them?"

"No."

"Suppose they ate all the strawberries and all the bananas? Then would you?"

"No."

"Suppose they ate all the strawberries and all the bananas and then attacked Daddy? Then would you?"

"No."

Drummer's forehead puckered.

"That's dumb. I would. I want to be just like Daddy."

Mandy looked down at her little brother. His uncombed

hair twisted in all directions like cypress twigs, and his brown eyes stared thoughtfully. She loved this brother so much. They had raised a baby marsh rabbit together, mended a mockingbird's wing, and watched the otter family dive in and out of the limestone holes on Trumpet Hammock. Now he was growing up and practicing to be a man by talking big about hunting.

They went in silence to the top of the steps.

"Are you going to write something else for the paper, Mandy?" he asked. "You do write good stories."

"I don't think so," she said. "I'm very busy now."

"Really?"

"I have a new friend."

"What's her name?"

"Nina Terrance."

"Is she pretty?"

"Cute, I'd say."

"I've never heard of her. Does she go to our school?"

"No. Her mother is very protective of her. She goes to a private school. I only see her at the dentist's office. She has braces, too."

"If you only see her at the dentist's office, how come you're so busy?"

"Well . . . I help with her favorite charity. She's rich."

"Guess you don't want to come catchin' frogs, then."

"No, I guess not." Mandy opened the door to her room, recalling Jack's criticism of her story. "Nuts," she said and flung herself on the bed to bury her face and cry as she had done after every other rejection. But no tears came. She was thinking of Nina Terrance.

2
The Bedroom

Later that afternoon Kray, the leader of the Trumpet Hammock crows, flew over Piney Woods and, spotting black feathers on the ground, focused acutely on them by rounding the curvature of his eye lens as crows do.

He dropped down on a tree limb near the skirted sable palm and stared. Unlike people, who have one central point of sharp vision, birds have two—one in the center of the retina and one in the rear. These, together with his overall crow vision, gave Kray three simultaneous views of the feathers, from each side and forward. What he saw said: "murdered crow."

"Nevah, nevah," he mourned. His cry traveled through the forest, rolled out over the saw grass, and penetrated the dark niches and hollows of Trumpet Hammock.

At the sound every crow froze where it was. It was as if

none existed. Extensions on stubs appeared, however, black knots on limbs, but no crows. They had become one with the inanimate things of the forest.

Nina Terrance heard Kray's doomsday pronouncement and looked at him through a hole in the leaves. Her stomach pinched with hunger; her legs wobbled from lack of nourishment. She needed only to cry the begging note of the eyas crow and Kray, or any other nearby crow, would drop down and feed the orphan, but she was rendered silent by his "sad crow" cry.

Still eyeing the black feathers, Kray sidled along the limb, then walked up a bough like a shadow. When he reached the top of the tree he spread his wings. A wind gusted under them, lifted him, and carried him sideways toward the hammock.

"Nevah, nevah," he moaned once more, then called sharply, "Caia," for crows call "caw" when they are flying away from their roost, "caia" when they are coming home.

An hour of silence passed, then the birds began to move again.

Nina Terrance turned her head. A beetle crept along the fingerlike edges of one of the palm leaves that made her nest. She watched it, but she was still unable to coordinate beak and eye to catch it. She had, however, today fanned her wings for the first time. Yesterday she had run her beak across her back feathers. Each day she could do one more bird skill as she developed toward being a bird that could fly.

When at sunset Kray announced the end of the day with one clear "Caw," the eyas shook herself and nestled down in her Mandy-made nest. Her hunger was unbearable. She

17

closed her eyes and slowed down her breathing to conserve energy.

Promptly at sunup, when she could see, she flopped to the edge of the nest and prepared to fling herself to the ground and cry until the crows of Trumpet Hammock came and fed her.

Crunch da dum. She could not move. The sound of the hunter's footsteps immobilized her. *Crunch da dum, crunch da dum.* Far away now, *crunch da dum.*

The sun touched the top of the pines and Kray announced the start of the day. His clan awoke and yawned, then silently preened their feathers to make them airtight for flight. The eyases in well-hidden nests opened their eyes. One was old enough to shake himself, three days more advanced than Nina Terrance.

Presently an adult crow designated himself guard crow for the morning, for the crows rotate this duty. He sailed to a stub on an old cypress tree, where he scanned the river of grass, the distant highway, Waterway Village, and the strawberry field. The berries matured later than most of Florida's strawberry crop, for they were a unique cross between a wild strawberry of the north and the enormous cultivated berries of Florida and California. Their flavor was piquant and sugar sweet, and they were very much in demand in fancy restaurants. The guard crow did not even glance at them. The "sad crow" call of yesterday had linked death to the woods.

The door of the cinder-block house opened and Mandy came out. The guard crow knew her as he did her mother. He considered them both harmless "large rabbits" of the yard and paths and was unafraid of them.

"Caaa caa ca," he called to the clan—a signal that meant disperse and go hunt. One by one the crows flapped through the trees and coasted on partially extended wings out across the Glades, then beat their way toward the distant highway where they scouted for road kill. The guard bird watched them go, flattening his eye lens to keep them in focus three and four miles away. Then he glanced out of the back of his eyes and scanned for enemies: snakes, rats, owls, hawks, anything that might threaten the precious eyases.

When the crows were gone, the mockingbirds and wrens flew to their singing posts and announced ownership of their part of the forest edge.

Nina Terrance was listening to them when she felt Mandy push back the huge leaves and enter the sable palm tent.

"Hi, Nina Terrance," she said. "I can't stay long. I sneaked out of the house before Daddy got up, to feed you and to make sure you're all right." Cupping her hands, she lifted Nina out of her nest and placed her on the ground. Dipping a piece of cheese sandwich in a jar of milk, she held it out for Nina Terrance. The bird instantly recognized the offering as food although she had never seen bread and cheese before. She fluttered her wings and begged. Mandy stuffed her mouth and broke off another bite.

As Nina Terrance ate she changed the shape of her eye lenses from flat to round and back again. Then she blinked. Something was happening to her mind. Mandy was becoming her mother and she, Nina Terrance, was becoming Mandy. Her feathers in her bird mind were knitting into human clothing, her head was becoming covered with brown hair, and her wings were feeling like hands.

Mandy was being imprinted on her mind, because whoever feeds a baby bird is stamped upon its brain as a parent,
be it a mechanical toy bird or a little girl. The bird thereafter
considers itself to be like the toy or the human.

By the end of the feeding Nina Terrance was looking with
adoration at her mother, whom she now thought she resem-
bled. Her mother picked her up, held her close, and after
smelling her sweet feathers put her in the nest.

"Stay still until I come back," she said.

"Ay," croaked Nina Terrance, fluttering her throat to
effect an imitation of her mother's voice.

When Mandy reached home her father was at his desk
in the living room making notes in his account book. He
struggled, head down, shoulders rounded over the work, for
Fred Tressel had never completed sixth grade and arithme-
tic came hard to him. He was only comfortable when he was
out in the greenhouse or field crossbreeding his famous stock
of strawberries and, when a good strain came along, an
occasional tomato or pepper. Mandy's mother, Barbara,
often said Fred Tressel was related to the pollinating bee.

Mandy paused on a dark step to watch this huge man who
had grown up planting vegetables and fruits—and also hunting alligators until they were protected by the National Park.
When he smiled, which was most of the time, he did not
seem like a person who could shoot crows. Once Mandy had
asked him why he did it, and he had answered: "My family
comes first. Our crops are our living."

This had not been a very satisfactory answer for Mandy
because, one, she had never seen a crow in the strawberry

patch, and two, crows were small and helpless like Nina Terrance.

She must ask him again, she thought as she crawled back into bed with her clothes on and waited until she heard her father fixing his breakfast in the kitchen below.

The clank of pans was her usual signal to get up. She arose, brushed her hair, and listened as she did every morning to Jack and Carver shouting in the shower and banging doors. In the cacophony of morning in the Tressel home she ran down the stairs and hurried through the living room and across the hall to her parents' room.

Her mother was seated at her dressing table brushing her short brown hair and coaxing the front curls into waves.

"Hi, honey," she said upon seeing Mandy in the mirror. "You look like you've swallowed an alligator. What's up?"

The door banged as her father went out to the strawberry field. Mandy sat down on the bed and patted the green slacks and shirt her mother had laid out for herself. She worked weekdays at the Agricultural Experiment Station at the north end of town.

"I have a new friend," she said.

"That's wonderful. What's her name?" Her mother peered closer at herself and rubbed a freckle on her cheek.

"Nina Terrance."

"That's an interesting name. Is she Puerto Rican?"

"No."

"Too bad, I hoped maybe she could help me. Maria and Teresa will be helping with the strawberry crop again and I can't always understand them."

"You speak good Spanish, Mommy," said Mandy,

smoothing the collar of the shirt on the bed.

"Well, I'm learning, but I could use help. And I hoped your new friend . . ."

"Nina Terrance can't possibly help," Mandy said so forcibly that Barbara looked again at her daughter's reflection in the mirror.

"I just wondered if she could, that's all. What color is your friend's hair?"

"Black."

"And her eyes?"

"A pale milky blue."

"Pale milky blue? Good heavens, Mandy, she sounds odd." Barbara Tressel slowly swung around on her stool and peered at her daughter. "What do her parents do?" she asked suspiciously.

"Fly."

"They do? Where does she live?"

"In Piney Woods."

"Oh, Mandy. Are you sure you should keep this friend?"

Mandy slid off the bed and walked to her mother's side.

"Yes, Mommy. I am."

"You know how your dad feels about crows?" She looked directly into Mandy's eyes. "I mean how he *really* feels about them."

"Yes."

"And you think you should go ahead with this?"

"I'll keep her out of his sight in the woods."

Barbara slowly brushed her hair.

"Where are her parents?"

"Dead. All the crows of Piney Woods are dead. Daddy

and Jack and Carver shot them all—all but Nina Terrance."

Barbara winced.

"I think you ought to talk to your father about this. He might not be as terrible as you think."

"But he is. He shoots crows."

"He also knows a lot about crows and might be able to help you. He says crows are vindictive and remember forever the persons who shoot at them. You wouldn't want that crow hurting Daddy or Jack or Carver, would you?"

Mandy did not answer.

"Maybe your dad knows how to erase an imprint of a killer in a crow's mind. Then it wouldn't hurt anyone."

"How could a crow possibly hurt anyone? Nina Terrance is small and gentle."

Barbara shrugged and changed the subject.

"Have you written any more stories?"

Mandy was about to say no, then changed her mind.

"One. For *The Waterway Times.*"

"Good. Are they going to run it?"

"No."

"Shoot," said Barbara with feeling. "Older brothers sure can be difficult. I had three."

Mandy's head drooped, and she took her mother's hand.

"Why won't they let me be part of the newspaper? Drummer is and he's just a little boy."

"I don't know, Mandy. I really don't know." She ran her fingers through Mandy's hair. "But I think it is something about practicing being dominant so they can compete out in the world. Soon Jack and Carver will have to seek their fortunes, so to speak."

"I do want to be a reporter for them. They have such a good time working together on that paper."

"Never mind, Mandy. You're wonderful."

"I'm not. I'm lonely. Loners don't grow and learn. I'll stay dumb." She slipped her arm around her mother and buried her face in her breast. Barbara hugged her.

"But you have a remarkable friend now in Nina Terrance."

Mandy blinked back her tears and smiled up at her mother.

"Nina Terrance attends a private school," said Mandy.

"Wow, she must be rich."

"Very rich. She has a favorite charity."

"She does?" Barbara knitted her brow trying to figure out where the game was leading.

"Yes, a poor family on the other side of Piney Woods."

"Oh, I see," Barbara nodded. "We must pack food boxes for them."

"Exactly," said Mandy, clapping her hands in the excitement of their fantasy world. "And she can't visit me. Her parents are very protective."

"Of course." Barbara squeezed Mandy's hand. "I would never have thought of that."

"I met her in the dentist's office. She has braces too."

"That's getting pretty complicated. Do you have to have met her in the dentist's office?"

"I've already told Drummer I did."

"Well, we had better stick with that. What else did you tell him about her?"

"That's all." Mandy threw herself back on the bed again. "Except that she's rich and has a charity."

"Good." Barbara became silent as if weighing the wisdom of Mandy's keeping the crow.

"How can I tell which is the alarm cry?" Mandy had sensed her change of heart and was trying to get her more involved. It worked.

"Watch old Kray, the boss bird that Drummer named," Barbara said. "I don't know which one he is, but your daddy says when he or Jack or Carver come near Trumpet Hammock, he gives the alarm cry and all his clan vanishes from sight."

"Does he give it when we come out?"

"No. He knows they hunt and kill crows and we don't." Barbara was smiling helplessly at her daughter. "Mandy, I'm such a sucker for this. Shall we pack a nice charity box for Nina Terrance's poor family?"

"You're going to play," Mandy exclaimed happily. "Oh, Mommy, you're going to love Nina Terrance."

"Yes, I'm afraid I am. Crows are fascinating, but you'll have to keep this one away from the farm."

"I can do it."

"Well, baby crows like to follow the parent that feeds them. You'll have to be clever. Doctor Bert, at the Experiment Station, is an expert on crows, too. I'll ask him what to do today and bring you some of the bulletins he writes about their behavior and food habits. Crows are social birds—that is, they live and work together like we people do. They are very intelligent, too. Your dad says they can even count. If three hunters go into a woods where a roost is, and two of them leave, the crows won't appear until the third hunter departs."

"Daddy would want me to play with an intelligent friend, wouldn't he?"

Barbara laughed and buttoned her shirt. "He certainly would."

3
"I Got Youv"

For the next ten days Mandy fed Nina Terrance before her father got up, on her way to the bus stop, at lunchtime, and three times between the final school bell and dusk. Doctor Bert had said that a parent crow would feed a nestling about once every hour, and more often than that just before they flew from the nest. With each feeding Mandy was more firmly imprinted on Nina Terrance's brain. At the sound of her footfall the eyas fluttered her wings. When the girl appeared in the leaf tent under the sable palm tree, Nina opened her mouth and cried out for food. Her feathers grew strong and shiny on the cheese, meat, and fruit plus the daily vitamin pill Barbara mashed into a hard-boiled egg yolk.

Each day saw her performing another achievement on the way to becoming a mature bird. At the end of the week she could stretch both wings down and hop on both feet as well as walk.

After feeding Nina one afternoon Mandy walked the short distance from the sable palm to the edge of Piney Woods and looked across the Glades to Trumpet Hammock. The crows were calling and "talking," and she was determined to try to decode their messages. Several times they cawed twice and were silent, and Mandy wondered if that was the alarm cry. She went back to Nina Terrance.

"CAW, CAW," she rasped. Nina simply cocked her head and yelled for food.

"Well, that's not it," she said and tossed a leaf to Nina, which she snagged with her foot and bit.

On a bright morning several days later Mandy made a strange breakthrough. She was wearing her sunglasses pushed back on her head like the eyes of a gigantic ant. Scurrying to the reading room on her hands and knees, she stood up so suddenly she terrified Nina Terrance.

"I got youv!" the crow said in a tense, high-pitched voice and jumped on Mandy's head, her eyes wide with terror.

Mandy peered through the leaves out into the woods to see who had spoken, although she knew perfectly well who it was. No one but Nina and herself were in the woods, and she had not spoken. She held out her wrist, and when Nina Terrance stepped on it, Mandy brought her down to eye level.

"You spoke," she said, her flesh tingling.

The eyas crow cocked her head and listened to Mandy's voice, then fluttered the feathers on her throat. A humanlike babble came out.

"Nina!" exclaimed Mandy. "You scare me."

The bird roused by lifting her feathers and shaking them, to say once more, "I like you and am at ease." Mandy stroked Nina Terrance's beak and gently straightened a twisted wing feather. A shot rang out from the far end of the strawberry field.

"Oh, no," said Mandy covering her ears.

"I got youv!" yelled Nina Terrance. Mandy drew her to her breast. Someone had taught Nina Terrance these words. She thought she recognized the voice, but when and why and who? Pushing her lunch box with her foot, Mandy put the crow on the ground and stroked her head. She calmed down rather quickly. Bird fears are short-lived. Knowing her food came in the green box, Nina Terrance hammered the lid with her beak. It gave no food. Drawing back her head, she cocked her eye and studied the latch. Then she leaned down and with a twist of her beak she opened it. She fell backward, the contents spilled out, and after regaining her balance she pecked the paper around a fish cake.

"Hey!" said Mandy. "You're getting too smart. Doctor Bert told Mommy I must keep you helpless if you are to be my pet." She dropped the fish back in the box and held out one bite.

"And he said," she went on, "I must always feed you, never let you eat on your own. That way I will keep you a baby and you won't be able to leave your nest. As long as you are a baby you'll stay where I put you." She fed the bird again.

When Mandy had stuffed Nina Terrance to silence, she placed her back in the nest, crawled out of the leaf tent, and hurried home. Her father was at his desk.

Mandy slipped past him, burst into her parents' bedroom, and rolled onto the unmade bed.

"Mom," she said with such force that Barbara turned away from the closet to look at her.

"What's the matter with you? You're pale."

"Can crows talk?"

"Yes. In a sense. You've heard your daddy say they have a variety of sounds—warning caws, assembly calls, and some very subtle ones like 'dying crow' calls and 'love duets.' "

"No, I mean English. Can they speak English?"

"English?"

"English."

Barbara sat down on her dressing table stool and stared at Mandy.

"Well," she said thoughtfully, "I read that crows will learn to imitate the human voice if words are repeated over and over again, just like parrots or myna birds. Why?"

"Nina Terrance jumped on my head and said, 'I got youv.' And I never said that to her in her life."

"I'll be darned," said Barbara rubbing her chin. "I guess Doctor Bert is right. He said the birds that imitate people's words—crows, ravens, parrots and myna birds, even starlings—will learn whole sentences when frightened badly enough at the time they hear the words. Konrad Lorenz, the famous animal behaviorist, wrote about his brother's parrot. The parrot was frightened by a soot-covered chimney sweep on the roof. Birds are very apt to be frightened by dark things above them because dark hawks and falcons get up above prey to dive and kill. One day the parrot shouted: 'The chimney sweep is coming, the chimney sweep is coming,' in the voice of the cook. She had apparently yelled the sentence months before just as the young man had climbed to the chimney and stood like a black killer above the bird." Mandy listened with widening eyes.

"And Lorenz knew a hooded crow called Hansl," Barbara went on. "It was the pet of a railwayman. The bird flew away and after a long absence returned home with a broken toe. His master and Lorenz wondered how this crow had hurt himself. One day the crow shouted in a lower Austrian dialect what would be, when translated into a Lancashire dialect, 'Got 'im in t'bloomin' trap,' and the culprit was revealed . . . an animal trapper three blocks away."

Mandy shook her head, delighted by the justice of it all. "I hope they punished him," she said. "I wonder who scared Nina Terrance?" she asked.

"I'll bet she heard someone shout 'I got youv' when the terrible gun blast killed her parents and knocked her out of the nest. Does the voice sound like anyone?"

"A little, but I don't know who."

4
Trumpet Hammock

One Sunday morning Mandy got up earlier than usual and, pulling on her blue jeans, stood at the window watching the mist rise. During the dry season of winter in southern Florida, the mist kept the plants alive by drenching them. Mandy saw it settle on the fronds of the coconut palm, forming balls of dew that rolled together and streamed down the leaf stem to the trunk.

The backyard mockingbird flew to the rivulet and drank. The frogs croaked in the moisture and the spiderwebs, silver with dew, shone like small carpets far out over the grasses of the Glades.

Sneaking quietly to the lookout post, this morning's guard crow checked the landscape for enemies, then announced the sunrise. The tribe awoke, yawned, scratched, and smoothed their feathers for flight.

"Caaa caa ca," the guard stated. Two crows left the Hammock in response to the "go hunt" signal. The mist was dense over the Glades, however, and they swung back to Piney Woods. Alighting on a tree near the banana patch, they waited for the sun to burn off the mist.

"Ca! Ca! Ca! Ca!" screamed the guard crow. Mandy clutched the window frame and leaned far out to see what the crows would do now. She thought this was the alarm cry, although she was not certain. The two vanished as if they had been erased. One flattened into the leaves, the other simply readjusted his feathers, caught the sun like a mirror, and changed into a patch of shadow and sunlight.

"That's *it*," she exclaimed. "That's the alarm cry. Now to learn to imitate it correctly and keep Nina Terrance away from the house. She understands that call. The first day I found her she cringed and sat still when Kray called four sharp cas."

Mandy put on a T-shirt with a pink flamingo painted on it by Drummer, picked up her walking boots, and tiptoed down the steps in her bare feet. Moving quietly to the refrigerator, she took out some turkey and corn, and she got a piece of cake from the cake box. Suddenly the back door opened.

"Hey," Drummer said, startled to see her. "What are you doing up so early?"

"Nina Terrance and I are going on a picnic," she answered, placing the food in her lunch box. "What are *you* doing up?"

Drummer walked to the refrigerator and helped himself.

to a big red strawberry. He popped it in his mouth and licked his lips.

"Yum," he said. "They're better this year than last."

"Where have *you* been?" Mandy asked.

"Fishing. Over at the village. I got a nice mess. Want some for breakfast?"

Mandy hesitated. She had planned to learn more crow talk this morning, but the idea of a breakfast with Drummer sounded wonderful.

"Sure," she said and put down her lunch box.

Drummer rolled the cleaned fish in cornmeal and dumped them in a pan of melted butter, then fried them to a golden crisp. Mandy set the table and they sat down together, content with each other's nearness.

"It wasn't the distributor," Drummer said as if the subject of the SAAB had never been dropped.

"Really? How do you know? Did it stop again?"

Drummer nodded. "Dead as a poisoned rat. Over at the high school. Some big guys helped us push it home."

"What's the trouble now?"

"Fuel pump. Carv thinks it's in the fuel system this time."

"Another edition of *The Waterway Times*?" Mandy asked.

"As soon as the strawberries are picked. Want to write for it this time? If you wrote a poem I could illustrate it and then they'd have to print it."

"Oh, Drummer." Mandy smiled at her little brother. "I guess I just can't write what Jack and Carver want. I've given up."

Drummer glanced at her with sad eyes. "Don't give up. You write good, Mandy."

"Nina Terrance and I are pretty busy these days," she explained.

"But I've found the barred owls. I know where their nest is. They should have eggs pretty soon and then little owlets. I'll get one, you can write a poem about it, and I'll draw their picture."

"I don't want to."

"The owls will be cute, Mandy," Drummer said, making a rather feeble last sales pitch. They lapsed into silence. The clock ticked loudly. Outside, the sun brightened the lawn and trees. Mandy picked out the fish bones with her fingers. She could imagine the pleasure of writing a poem about owls, but she would not write it.

Jack came into the kitchen, yawned, and rubbed his eyes. After glancing at Drummer and Mandy he turned toward his room and yelled in a voice loud enough to be heard at Waterway Village: "Carv, get out of bed. We've got to pick today."

Jack crashed a frying pan onto the stove, Carver's door banged open, the shower thundered, and the water pump started up. The house rocked with the activities of the young Tressel men.

In the midst of the din Fred Tressel came into the kitchen, said hello to Mandy, gave Drummer a chuck on the cheek, and peered hungrily at Jack's scrambled eggs.

"Have the pickers come?" he asked him.

"Not yet."

"They should be here." He turned to the kitchen telephone and Mandy gathered up her dishes and rinsed them in the sink. Barbara arrived dressed for work in the field.

"Where are you going?" she asked.

"Nina Terrance and I are having a picnic."

"That's nice, but don't stay too long. I'll need some help with the crating."

"Who's Nina Terrance?" asked Fred. Mandy looked to her mother for support, for she had never lied to her father before. Barbara had her back turned and was squeezing oranges.

"Some new girl," answered Jack. "Her father's the new city planner, Pierce Terrance."

Mandy's mouth opened, her neck stretched like a curious crane.

"What's a city planner?" Fred asked and cracked some eggs for his own breakfast. "Don't stay long, Mandy. Your mother needs you."

When Mandy arrived at the fork in the path, she found Nina Terrance sitting in the middle of the trail.

"Nina, not on the path!" she screamed and grabbed her. "Get off." Gathering Nina to her breast she felt her go into shock, tense, and lie still.

"Nina," she cried, cradling her in her arms and stroking her gently. The fingering sent the crow into a deeper trance. Mandy carried her to the sable palm, pushed back the two big fronds that formed the door, and crawled to the nest room. She stirred the dry leaves and they snapped like casta-nets.

"Caw caw caw," she rasped, imitating the ordinary caws of the crows that she heard every day. "I didn't mean to scare you," she added. Nina Terrance did not move, for the stroking had hypnotized her. Now through the haze of this strange state of mind she heard Mandy whisper: "It's okay. It's okay." The voice was reassuring. Nina Terrance rolled to her feet and stood up. Blinking her eyes, she quickly oriented herself and begged for food.

"Hey," Mandy said. "When I said 'okay' you came out of your trance. You not only speak English, you understand it. Maybe I won't have to learn crow talk after all."

Mandy raised her hands above her head and pounced once more toward Nina Terrance while shouting at her. The crow did not go into a trance.

"You know I'm acting, don't you?" she said. She laughed and tried again, this time trying to scare herself with a vision of Old Monster, the six-foot alligator. More annoyed than frightened, Nina Terrance hunched down.

"Okay," said Mandy, and Nina Terrance stood up and roused.

"So far so good," mused Mandy, then said aloud to Nina, "Maybe I can keep you away from the yard and the strawberry patch by scaring you. You've got to listen to me, or you'll get shot."

Nina Terrance walked past Mandy as she sat cross-legged on the ground. Waddling slightly, tilting mischievously, she kept her rear focal point on her child-mother's face, then swift as a dragonfly pecked open Mandy's shoelace. With a twist the bow fell apart.

As Mandy reached to tie it, Nina hopped a few inches off the ground, beat her wings, and dropped to the earth beside the lunch box. She clutched the latch in her beak and flipped it open. Using her whole body for a lever, she lifted the lid and looked in.

Mandy dropped to her knees and grabbed the cake and turkey, but not before Nina Terrance had picked up the corn.

"Ca! Ca! Ca! Ca!" Mandy rasped a crowlike noise by holding her nose. This time Nina looked nervous.

"*I* must feed you, not you," Mandy scolded. "I have to keep you a baby or you'll fly to the farm and get killed." She pulled on the cob, but Nina would not let go.

Mandy loomed over the young crow. "Ca! Ca! Ca! Ca!" Mandy held her nose again and sharpened her cry. Nina Terrance dropped the corn and crouched low. She did not move a feather.

"Okay," Mandy said. Nina stood up and Mandy fed her until she was almost full. Then she offered the cake. Nina devoured it with soft swallowing noises, and feathers lifted, she climbed up Mandy's arm. When she reached her shoulder Nina Terrance sat down.

"Ay, ay, okay, okay," Nina said quite clearly.

Getting carefully to her feet so as not to loosen the crow's grip, Mandy stole through the leaf corridor to the door.

"We are going to Trumpet Hammock today," she said. "I'm going to learn the dispersal call. I can make you lie still with the alarm call; now I want to make you fly off when I shout from far away, like Doctor Bert's research papers say the dispersal call will do. In that way we're covered for most emergencies."

Mandy came to the end of Piney Woods and started into the saw grass. The jagged edges of the tough sedge ripped at her pants and scratched her boots. She was glad she had dressed for the Glades.

With the crow riding contentedly on her shoulder, she crossed through the winter-dry swampland to Trumpet Hammock. A moat dug by alligators surrounded the island of hardwood trees. At its brink Mandy paused and looked to the right and left. Old Monster, the six-foot-long alligator, lived here. Her father had warned her never to cross into the hammock without knowing where he was. "He can move faster than a pig's squeal," he had said. "And chomp you to bits."

Old Monster was lying under a fig tree on the bank, a safe fifty feet away. Holding out her arms to balance herself, Mandy crossed the log her brothers had felled for a bridge and entered the shadows of Trumpet Hammock.

Ancient oak and bustic trees twined upward and leafed against the sky like a roof. Only a few shafts of sunlight entered the forest. Bromeliads and orchids festooned the limbs like pineapple tops. Ferns grew in the damp soil; warblers sang and insects darted and hummed.

Mandy loved Trumpet Hammock, for it reminded her of a beautiful greenhouse; but she never made a habit of visiting it because of the snakes. She imagined them everywhere in this jungly habitat—water snakes, swamp snakes, hognose snakes, green snakes, corn snakes, and worst of all the deadly coral and cottonmouth snakes. Gingerly she stepped over red flowers and slats of ferns as she peered up into the trees for a crows' nest. When she found one she planned to climb the tree, make the crows frantic, and listen to them shriek the dispersal call. Snakes or no, she must protect Nina Terrance from the hunters.

She could see no sign of a nest, not a feather or splash of bird whitewash. The crows were secretive when they had young. Even her father had never found a crows' nest in Trumpet Hammock. He had found them in Piney Woods by sitting under a saw palmetto and waiting until the birds came home with food in their mouths to feed their young. The Trumpet Hammock birds were too smart even for Fred.

Most crows nest in pine trees, but when the Tressels had bought the swamp-edge farm years ago and begun their war on the birds, a few of the most intelligent moved into Trumpet Hammock and thrived, their nests undetected among the vines and air plants and leaves.

Mandy, with Nina Terrance balancing on her shoulder, circled a well-like sinkhole leached out of the limestone by rain and plant acids. She came to a halt under a live oak thinking that she saw a crows' nest high in the limbs. By standing directly beneath it she could see it was only a huge clump of ball moss.

After checking for snakes she sat down on a log to wait as her father had. Nina Terrance made a soft sound and gently nuzzled her beak in her hair. A warbler flew down to take a few of the insects that began to swarm around the pair; a spadefoot toad grumped and came closer.

Suddenly Nina Terrance flattened her feathers and cocked her head. She was focused on something above her. Mandy looked up but saw only bromeliads and moss. Nina Terrance dug in her toes and her eye pinned, Mandy thought, on a dead bromeliad. Then the light shifted, the plant moved, and she saw it to be Kray. She recognized him by his head. According to her father the center feathers were permanently creased by a bullet. Mandy sat so still a butterfly alighted on her; but Kray was not looking at her. He was intent upon Nina Terrance. The two birds stared at each other. Kray was disconcerted by the sight of a crow with a person. His throat feathers pumped and the sad call of "Nevah, nevah," slipped from him.

A limb crotch behind his head, covered with ferns and a huge spider orchid, began to move and change shape. Four little crows appeared.

"A nest!" Mandy gasped. "And the babies are your age, Nina Terrance. They still have head down, too."

As Mandy planned a route up the tree, Nina Terrance sat down on her shoulder and pecked her ear.

"You're not interested anymore, are you?" she said. "Of course not. They're crows and you think you're a person." She snuggled her head against the warm crow and smiled at the strangeness of the bird mind.

As she studied the tree more crows came out of the shadows to look at Nina Terrance. They appeared like the creatures on the rubbings she and her mother had made in an old Spanish church; an eye here, a foot, and then a whole animal. Because Mandy sat so still, other wild things appeared. An egret stretched its neck. A woodpecker flew past and landed on the trunk of a nearby bustic tree.

Then she saw the barred owl on a limb beyond the woodpecker. His eyes were half closed and he was slowly turning his head as he perceived the forest waking up while he fell asleep.

His feathers were filmy and beautifully marked, his pensive face was round like a pale moon. Immediately a poem came to Mandy's mind.

"Caaaw! Caaaw! Caaaw! Caaaw! Caaaw," the guard crow screamed as he saw the owl. "Assemble around the owl." The call rolled out over the Glades and the crows in the saw grass heard and winged into action. Dropping into the hammock along secret routes among the limbs, beating their wings, dodging twigs that could poke out their eyes, they enthusiastically answered the summons to harass the owl.

"Caaaw! Caaaw! Caaaw! Caaaw! Caaaw! Eva, ha!" ("The owl is off its nest. Get the owlets, get the owlets. Harass! Kill! Kill!") They hated owls. Owls kill and eat young crows.

When the crows were mobbed around the owl, one took off for the owl's nest to stab its eggs or young, whichever it found. Every crow knew where the nest was and waited for an opportunity to catch the parents away. As the would-be murderer slunk along he saw the female on the nest, her wings spread, her head stretched out on the sticks, staring ominously back at him. Nothing could be done. The young were safe beneath her. The crow returned to mob her mate, continuing a feud between owl and crow as ancient as the forest itself.

Mandy watched in fascination and even Nina Terrance was excited by this show. Within her, inherited instincts stirred. She focused on the barred owl, clamped her feathers to her body, and yelled a brisk "Okay," then became silent.

The harassment continued. Two crows dove at the owl, coming closer and closer. One struck him with his wing. Unable to put up with this anymore, the owl took off. He flew directly above Mandy and Nina Terrance.

"I got youv!" screamed Nina Terrance. At the sight of the hunter overhead she had responded with the only alarm cry she knew how to yell.

"I got youv!" she yelled again.

Kray heard the voice of the human hunter.

"Ca! Ca! Ca! Ca!" he cried in alarm.

A silence descended upon the hammock jungle and every crow vanished from sight.

"Ca! Ca! Ca! Ca!" Mandy imitated, holding her nose. Nina Terrance hunkered down on her shoulder and froze.

After a long time Mandy whispered, "Okay," and Nina Terrance relaxed and stood up.

"We've got it!" exclaimed Mandy. "The alarm cry works!"

Happily she got to her feet and, again keeping an eye out for snakes, wound among the trees toward the log bridge.

"Caw!" pronounced Kray. Mandy stopped and glanced back. One at a time the crows of Trumpet Hammock sought out their aerial avenues that twisted among the limbs and went off to hunt the Glades.

"Now, why did they go hunting when Kray gave one caw? I hear him say that at night just as the sun goes down. That means 'good night.' Now it seems to mean 'all clear!' Mommy's right, there are two different meanings for the same sound."

Mandy looked down at Nina Terrance. "Cak-ca," she said, inventing a soft sound to express her affection for the bird.

"Cak-ca," answered Nina Terrance and relaxed her feathers.

"Good girl," said Mandy. "We can reassure each other

now. Cak-ca, that's our talk. It means everything's all right, love ya."

Old Monster was swimming down the middle of the moat, his eyes and nose just above the surface of the water. She waited until he had drifted under the footbridge. He swung his tail from side to side as he slowly submerged in a deep pool where his favorite foods, garfish and snapping turtles, lived. When his nose and eyes sank out of sight, Mandy ran over the log into the saw grass.

Nina rode on her shoulder until they reached Piney Woods; then she jumped to the ground and, standing tall, exercised her wings by flapping them vigorously.

"You'll soon be a fledgling," Mandy said. "You can stand on your toes and fan your wings; you can run and perch, freeze and watch prey. Now I want you to listen to me." Picking her up, she tucked her under her arm and crawled under the sable palm's leaves to their room.

"Ca! Ca! Ca! Ca!" she said. Nina sat down on her heels immediately. The palm leaves cast fingerlike shadows over her blackness and she became one with the pattern of the tree. Satisfied that both she and Nina Terrance were ready for the fledgling stage of crow life, Mandy went on all fours out of the hideout and hurried home to help her mother.

Maria and Teresa were working in the fields with Fred, Jack, and Carver. All were kneeling in the warm sun picking the huge ripe berries that would be wrapped individually and flown north to fancy restaurants in New York City, Chicago, and Boston. Famous restaurateurs placed orders a year in advance for Fred Tressel's huge strawberries with the flavor of wild ones.

Maria and Teresa sang and talked as they worked; her brothers and father listened and smiled. The smell of the strawberries was sweet on the air and Mandy felt the excitement of harvesting the Tressel family's famous crop. She ran down the path to the gate and around the shed to the table under the fig tree.

"Can I help?" she asked.

"You most certainly can," Barbara answered. "How's Nina Terrance?"

"Just fine. She sends her love." Mandy's eyes sparkled.

"Drummer!" called her mother as she saw him run around the house and duck behind the jasmine tree. "Come help."

Pleased to be considered old enough, he came out of hiding and hurried to the table.

"Watch." His mother placed a tissue in the palm of her hand, placed a huge glistening berry on it, twisted the ends of the paper, and placed the little package in a depression in a plastic container. Drummer imitated her and for the next hour worked with precision and diligence. Then he saw his father coming in from the field.

"Now that I am old enough to work," he said testily to his mother and Mandy, "maybe Daddy will change the rules about teaching us boys how to shoot. Maybe he'll teach me now, so I won't have to wait 'til I'm twelve."

"Are you really going to shoot a gun, Drummer?" Mandy gasped. "It's okay to be on Mommy's and my side. You don't have to hunt."

"I know," he said, but his eyes were upon his father, who was swinging home through the field.

5
"On the Path"

When Mandy crawled under the sable palm a few afternoons later, Nina Terrance spread her wings and flew twice around her head.

"You can fly!" she cried. "You're a grown-up bird. Now I must be very sure you don't learn to eat on your own or you'll fly to the farm." She fed Nina Terrance who, like all newly fledged birds, once stuffed with food sat down on her nest and fell asleep.

The following morning, however, as Mandy crawled out of the palm-tree house after feeding Nina Terrance her breakfast, the young crow walked out behind her.

"This won't do," she scolded and carried her back.

"Stay here," she admonished, then spanked her beak lightly with a leaf.

With that the young crow lowered her wings and dropped her head. A surly sound rumbled from her chest.

"Why, you're sulking," Mandy exclaimed. "I know you're sulking; that's just what I do when I pout; I sag my shoulders, bend my head, and go 'hmmmpf.' " Mandy rested her elbow in her hand and her fingers on her chin.

"You know, I'm beginning to understand how people figure out the behavior of animals. You act a lot like we do. When you're hungry you open your mouth and beg, when you're scared you cower down and sit stone still, and when you're mad you yell. So do I. Now you're sulking 'cause I scolded you. But Nina, please don't come out of the palm tent or you'll be shot." Mandy spanked her once more and departed. Nina did not follow.

With all the orders coming in, Fred had moved his office to the family room. He was working at the table when Mandy arrived. As she leaned over his shoulders to hug him, she noticed that the shotgun was out of the gun rack and standing in the corner by the door.

"What's the gun out for?" she asked.

"Crows," he answered and turned a page in his order book. "I can't take a chance now. The crop is coming on fast and good. I want every juicy berry."

"By the way," Mandy said, withdrawing, "I've never seen a crow in the strawberries, Daddy. Do they really eat them?"

"Mandy, gal, one thing I do know about is crows. Yes, they do, if they can. That old Kray out there in Trumpet Hammock would take every berry, except for one thing . . . I shoot crows. So he won't come on my property.

Now and then I take out the gun to remind him."

"You mean, he doesn't eat our berries because you simply carry a gun?"

"That's right. All you have to do is shoot a crow or two. Better yet, hang up a dead one if you don't want them around, and they get the message. After that they stay away, 'specially if they see you with a gun."

"All of them?"

"All of them."

"Even the ones in Piney Woods?"

"Well, they're not as smart, but they seem to be learning. I didn't get one last nest, and yet I haven't seen or heard a single crow from Piney Woods."

Mandy thought for a moment; if her father was right perhaps Nina Terrance already knew not to come to the farm. Perhaps she was safe after all.

"Except this morning, of course," her father went on, "when I was walking along with the gun and you hollered, 'On the path.' I turned and saw that crow you were yelling about, but do you think I could get him? Not a chance. Saw I'had the gun and whoosh—vanished."

"I said, 'On the path'?"

"Well, you sure did." He turned and looked at her, perplexed.

Mandy went to the sink and turned on the water to give herself time to think when she had said "On the path." A few days ago she had found Nina Terrance on the path and had pounced upon her. "Nina, not on the path!" she had shouted, frightening her badly enough to imprint on her mind part of a sentence. Mandy put her hand over her mouth to keep from giggling.

"Don't you remember?" he asked.

"Oh yeah, sure," she answered. Then to herself she said: "But not this morning." She filled a glass with water and drank it slowly. By the time it was empty she decided to tell him about Nina Terrance. Perhaps her mother was right. He might like this talking crow and become so intrigued with her he would not harm her. She turned around to speak; but no words came out.

Mandy gathered up her schoolbooks and started toward the attic steps. Her father got to his feet.

"It's good to talk to you," he said. "I haven't seen much of you lately. You go to school early and come home late. Is everything okay?"

"Yes," she answered, avoiding his eyes. "Everything is just right."

On the run across the yard to help her mother, she felt very pleased with herself. Having figured out the alarm cry of the crow, she now need never confront her father with her secret. She would live two lives: one in the woods with Nina Terrance, the other as an obedient daughter. The odor of strawberries perfumed the air beneath the fig tree and she breathed deeply.

A few hours later Barbara sent Mandy to the kitchen to put the ham in the oven for dinner and she was surprised to find her father still at the table. He was laboriously addressing the labels for the crates and checking them back with the order forms. It was his hour to be in the greenhouse. She offered to help, but he shook his head. The door swept open and Carver came in.

"That damned dog, Barney, nearly bit me again," he said. "I was delivering papers."

"He's a mean one," said Fred, looking up from his work. "A person shouldn't keep such an animal." He shook his head thoughtfully. "People come first."

"Hey, where's the gun?" Carver asked.

"You can't shoot that dog," Fred said.

"Not the dog. A crow. As I was coming through the woods I saw one on the path sneaking toward the strawberries."

Fred pointed to the corner. "There. Hey, no. It's gone. Who has it?"

"Not Jack. He was with me," said Carver.

"And Drummer certainly doesn't have it," said Fred. "Or does he?" He got to his feet.

Mandy bit her lip and hoped not. Her father was strict about the gun. The boys had to be twelve years old and have two or three months of intensive instruction before they could use one of the hunting guns. Jack had sneaked off with the .22 rifle when he was only eleven and was punished by having his gun lessons postponed for a whole year.

The gate creaked open and footsteps sounded on the path. All three looked out to see Jack coming, gun in hand. Mandy felt relieved that Drummer didn't have it.

"What's up?" Jack said, entering and looking at the theater of faces. "You all look as if you'd seen a flying saucer."

"The gun," said Fred. "I didn't see you take it."

"You were busy on the phone," said Jack, "and I decided to deliver the papers the only way possible with that dog around."

The door opened again and Drummer came in.

"Man, it was a great show." He was grinning broadly, his eyes bright. "Barney tore Jack's pants and Jack turned around, and *bang*, he got Barney's rear end with a load of rock salt. Barney howled and ran home." He laughed mischievously. "Then we delivered the papers."

Fred was about to speak, but Drummer was not finished.

"Look, Carv, we're rich." He held up a canvas bag and jingled the coins inside.

"Doesn't sound like enough to pay for a universal joint yet," said Carver. "One more edition."

"I should be giving you guys a lecture about shooting the neighbor's dog and taking the gun without permission, but I won't. I just got a letter from Cornell University asking me to come to Ithaca next month to be a consultant. They are trying to improve their strawberry breeding program."

"Dad, that's great," said Carver. "Cornell is one of the best agricultural schools in the world. Man, they want *you*?"

"Wow, you're famous," said Drummer. "Can we all go? Get out of school?"

"Maybe. I'll think about it. Seeing New York might be just what we ought to do with some of the strawberry money this year."

Drummer ran out the door yelling the news to his mother. Mandy followed. The two came up to the packing table just as Maria and Teresa arrived for their week's pay. Barbara opened the strongbox and took out their checks.

"Now put the money in the bank," she said in Spanish.

"You should have checking accounts so you can plan and budget your income."

"No, no," answered Maria, also in Spanish. "I must give it all to my husband."

"But it's yours," Barbara insisted.

"He gives me some . . . for the food." She looked at Barbara resignedly. "He is the man. That's how it is."

"You both should think about budgeting your money. You're very capable," said Barbara.

Maria glanced at Teresa and Mandy could see the pain of resignation on their faces. Tired, heads down, they started off to the road where they would wait for one of their husbands to pick them up; sometimes it was hours.

"I wish I could make them understand," Barbara said when they had departed. "They work so hard and so well, then turn their checks right over to their husbands. It makes me so mad."

Mandy studied her mother's face. She was not as mad as she was concerned. She cared about Maria and Teresa and truly wished to help them. She was even taking Spanish lessons so she could understand them better.

Early the next morning Mandy looked out the window to see her father patrolling the strawberry field in the shadowy mist. In his hand he carried the shotgun.

"Nina Terrance, lie low," Mandy whispered. Then she said to herself: "I ought to tell Drummer that Nina Terrance is a little crow. I could borrow his tape recorder and tape the alarm cry. I'd get Drummer to run a wire and speaker out to Piney Woods and when Daddy went out with the gun I'd push the button. 'Ca! Ca! Ca! Ca!'—four cas the tape would scream, and she would sit still."

Mandy watched her father round the field. No sounds came from Trumpet Hammock. Even the guard crow did not appear. Apparently her father was right—when he walked with a gun, not a crow showed itself.

Dressing hurriedly, she ran to her mother's room, dove into the bed, and wrapped the sheet around herself until only her eyes showed.

"Something is bothering you," said Barbara, recognizing Mandy's troubled pose. "What is it now?"

"When do young crows become independent and leave home . . . go far, far away?"

"When they're about three or four months, I think I heard your dad say, but I'm not sure. Why?"

"Daddy saw Nina Terrance on the path and he wants to shoot her. I know it was Nina Terrance because she was walking, like a person. The young crows of Trumpet Hammock fly like their parents."

"I hope she doesn't walk this way. Maybe someone else should feed her until your father stops patrolling . . . someone off the farm; in the village perhaps."

"How about Mrs. Howard? She loves birds and animals," suggested Mandy.

"That's a good idea. I do worry about that crow attacking one of our men."

"Oh Mommy, what on earth could she do? Hit them with a wing? Peck them? She really can't hurt a huge, big person."

"I guess not." Barbara's voice trailed off weakly. She was not entirely convinced.

"And do you know what else Nina Terrance does?" Mandy said, sitting up.

Barbara turned from the mirror to listen.

"That little crow spoke to Daddy. She said, 'On the path,' in my voice and he thought it was me." She pressed her hands together in the joy of the trickery. "He turned around and saw her but she skedaddled before he got the gun up." Mandy laughed. "Nina can say, 'I got you,' 'Okay,' and 'On the path.' Isn't that neat? We have a talking crow."

"We certainly do, and she is fooling the smartest crow hunter in Dade County . . . I hope. You are still not ready to confide in your dad?" Barbara's voice was soft but also clear and firm.

"No," said Mandy. "I'm on my way to see Mrs. Howard."

By the time Mandy and her mother were ready for breakfast, Fred and the boys had eaten, washed their dishes, and gone. Mandy packed a slice of leftover ham, some potato salad, and a piece of Key lime pie in the green lunch box. She picked up her books.

"Your dad is going to take you and the boys to New York," Barbara said.

"Aren't you going?" Mandy asked.

"Someone has to stay and keep an eye on the farm."

"Some two have to stay," Mandy said firmly.

Barbara smiled, picked up an orange, and, humming to herself, walked to the packing table to work a few hours before going off to the Experiment Station.

6
Barney

Mandy was relieved when the last strawberry was picked and shipped off to the north. Maria and Teresa helped only one day a week, digging up the old plants, burning them, and raking the soil for next year's crop. Each October new plants, carefully cultivated in the greenhouse, were placed in the ground.

The rainy season began in late May. After sunny bright mornings, white puffy clouds would form, pile into huge thunderheads, and pour rain in the late afternoon and night. The waters of the Glades began to rise, and the white egrets and wood storks hunted the grasses of the Everglades. Fish and small water animals flourished wherever there was water.

Fred Tressel put the gun in the gun rack and went to work in the banana patch. He cut down the old trees that had borne fruit and were dying and cleared the way for the new sprouts emerging from their roots. In the late afternoons he worked in the greenhouse selecting the seeds from the best strawberries of the year. These he grew, crossing their pollens to breed even finer plants.

Mandy felt very secure about Nina Terrance. She responded perfectly to the "Ca! Ca! Ca! Ca!" cry and had taken to visiting Waterway Village, not the farm. Mandy was glad she had not distressed her father by telling him about her crow. The time was close at hand for Nina to forget she was a person and fly off to new country with the young crows.

Mandy awoke late one Saturday morning to hear Jack and Carver wrenching steel and shouting orders as they took the transmission out of the SAAB. She hurried downstairs, packed the lunch box, and was walking out the door when she sensed that something was not quite right. She glanced around. The gun was gone.

"Dad!" she called to see if he were in the house. No answer.

"Dad!" It had to be him. Jack and Carver were working on the SAAB. Her father must have seen Nina Terrance on the path and gone off to shoot her. Flinging the door open, she jumped down the steps and ran full speed to Piney Woods, where she crouched down behind a clump of fanlike saw palmettos.

"Ca! Ca! Ca! Ca!" she rasped, holding her nose. "Ca! Ca! Ca! Ca!"

A cottontail rabbit sat tight in the grass at the warning

from the crows. A purple grackle stopped eating and looked around.

Crunch da dum. Crunch da dum. The footfall was light, as if her father had seen something and was stalking.

Crunch da dum. He had turned and was walking toward the road, away from Nina's hangouts. Mandy sat back on her heels.

The barred owl boomed his morning check-in call to his mate, who answered. A bobwhite sentinel not far from Mandy warned his covey not to come this way. He had seen her. The crows of Trumpet Hammock, on the other hand, were quiet, although this was their hour to "talk." Mandy was pleased. Her warning had worked for them as well as Nina Terrance.

Crunch da dum.

"Here comes that damn dog again!" Jack yelled to his father.

The crows were safely hiding. Mandy jumped up and ran to meet her father and brother. She went all the way down the trail to the edge of the woods but could not find them. She climbed a tree and looked around, then plunged through the pineland broom grass. She still could not find them.

The village, she thought. They have gone to visit someone. Mandy started to cross the golf course, but Barney barked and she decided to stay where she was. He came on, however, his lips curled back from his teeth, the hair on his back lifted to make him look bigger and more ferocious.

"Here comes that damn dog again!" Jack was up in a tree.

She grinned and looked up. There sat Nina Terrance.

"Nina!" Mandy exclaimed. "It's you." She held up her hand and Nina Terrance roused, shook herself and, raising her wings, floated to Mandy's fingers.

Crunch da dum. Crunch da dum. Nina flattened her feathers and drew up in terror.

"I got youv!" she screamed.

"It's okay. It's okay," Mandy whispered as the crow prepared to take off. The words carried her back into the hypnotic state and she quieted down, came out of the trance, and shook her feathers.

Barney was halfway across the golf course barking at them. Nina Terrance cocked her eye and focused on him from all three directions of her sight. Leaping onto her open wings, she took two deep flaps toward Barney, coasting within two feet of his nose. He leaped at her, closed his jaws on air, and fell on his chest. When he had regained his legs Nina Terrance was once more above him. The dog bellowed and plunged after her. With an upward thrust of her wings the crow moved just out of his grasp and winged across the golf course. Leaping and howling, Barney chased her.

She led him down to the road, around the far cluster of one-story apartments, through the coconut palm grove, past the swimming pool and the shuffleboard court. Barney's tongue hung long from his mouth and dripped perspiration as he came down the far side of the village. Mandy could not suppress her laughter.

Barney stumbled and fell, and Nina Terrance flew into the fig tree by Mrs. Howard's home. The dog saw she was out of reach and did not attempt to get up. Instead he lay on his side, gasping for breath in the hot sun. Just before he recovered, Nina Terrance swooped down and flew over his nose. Barney struggled to his feet and ran after her, yelping. He was a hunting dog compelled to chase. Off he went.

As they came around the apartments the second time Mandy was afraid Barney was going to have a heart attack. His voice rattled and his eyes rolled.

"Caaaw, caaaw, caaaw, caaaw"—Mandy rasped out the call to assemble and, holding up a fish sandwich, darted into the shelter of Piney Woods.

Nina followed her, dropping to her hand just as Mr. Hathaway banged out of his apartment. Barney howled to his master, sides heaving. The elderly man hustled to his dog, gathered him up in his arms, and carried him inside.

Mandy felt bad about Mr. Hathaway's distress for his dog, but she no longer held any affection for Barney. He had snapped at Carver, bitten Jack's trouser leg, and tried to kill Nina Terrance.

As Mandy turned to take Nina back to her nest under the sable palm, Betty Howard, her white hair freshly bobbed and combed, limped out of her apartment and toward the giant fig tree. Under it sat a sandbox for her great-grand-daughter, Meredith, when she visited, which was frequent. Putting down her cane, she picked up a rake and began to remove the leaves from the box. Mandy decided this was a good time to speak to her about helping with the crow's feeding.

She glanced at Nina Terrance's crop, now bulging with food. She would want to rest. Taking a pop top out of her pants pocket, she held it before the crow. Instantly Nina snatched the bright object and flew high into the pine tree, creeping out of sight as she searched out a private spot to play with it. Convinced that even her father could not find Nina, Mandy ran across the lawn to greet Betty Howard.

"I'll bet Meredith is coming," she said and leaned down to pick up some of the leaves.

"You're right. I hope you have time to read to her again."

"I sure do," Mandy answered pleasantly, for she did love to read to little four-year-old Meredith. "By the way, did you notice that crow leading Barney around the village?"

"And that's not the first time." Mrs. Howard straightened up and grinned. "That bird's going to kill Barney. I'd be all for it, except Alvin Hathaway is such a nice man and he loves that dog." Shading her eyes with her hand she peered up into the fig tree.

"That crow likes this fig tree. I see him here every morning. I think he just waits here for Barney to come out and then teases him."

"She's here every morning?"

"She? Is it a she? Can you tell the difference?"

"Well, no, not really. I call all birds 'she' and all dogs 'he' no matter what they are."

"Me too. And cats are all shes."

"She waits for Barney to come out?" Mandy changed the conversation back to Nina Terrance.

"For the last four or five days she has come here around ten and stayed until lunchtime. If Barney comes out she runs him ragged. Then she flies into the woods and comes back in the late afternoon. She roosts in my fig tree at night."

Mandy smiled to learn of Nina's habits, and changed her mind about asking Mrs. Howard to feed her. Nina Terrance was doing just what she and her mother hoped she would do, moving away from the farm.

"Caw," she said to herself. "All's well."

Mandy helped Mrs. Howard stuff the leaves in a plastic bag, and thought about the upcoming trip to New York for her brothers and father. While they were gone she would wean Nina, so when they returned she would be back with the crows. Suddenly she hated the whole idea of letting Nina go.

"Ask Drummer if he would like to help me assemble the new sliding board I bought for Meredith," Betty Howard said. "My hands are no good anymore." She opened and closed her arthritic fingers. "I would have asked him myself when I heard him out here this morning, but he left before I could speak to him."

"Drummer was here?"

"Yes. At the same time you were here, around ten. I heard you. Why didn't you come see me?"

"Oh," said Mandy slowly, giving herself time to think. "Well, I had to leave quickly to help Mom."

Mandy turned to go home, but Betty Howard stayed her with a hand on her arm. "Meredith will be here tomorrow, so if Drummer could come today?"

"You'd better telephone him," said Mandy. "I won't get home for an hour or so."

Mandy was anxious to find Nina Terrance and hear her speak like Drummer. Drummer! What had the crow learned from Drummer? She said good-bye and darted to the spot where she had left Nina Terrance playing with the pop top.

The crow had dropped to the ground and was hiding the top under a leaf. Mandy jumped to her side.

"On the path!" screamed the startled bird.

"That's me." She chuckled. "Now tell me what Drummer says." The young crow flew to her shoulder and fluttered like a baby bird.

"Awk," she said.

Mandy carried her back to the sable palm, and scurrying like a crab, she moved sideways to the reading room and sat down. The crow hopped to her knee, cocked her head, and roused.

"Say your lessons," Mandy said. "I've got to know what you learned from Drummer.

"On the path," she said to stimulate Nina Terrance to talk, but the bird preened her feathers and ignored her.

Mandy rolled onto her back and Nina Terrance walked down her chest, pecked the buttons on her trousers, flew to her shoe, and untied the laces.

"Say, 'That's perfect!' " Mandy said. " 'That's perfect. That's perfect.' " She repeated the phrase over and over, hoping to teach her by repetition, but Nina Terrance just cocked her head and tried to pull the ring off Mandy's finger.

"Oh, well," Mandy said, touching the vibrissae—the soft, hairlike feathers—at the base of Nina's beak. "I guess I'll never be a star reporter. I had hoped to put you in a tree above Jack's head when I show him my next story. Then when I say: 'How's this one?' you'll answer, 'That's perfect.' "

She laughed and flopped over onto her stomach.

"Ha, ha, ha. Very funny. Ha, ha, ha."

Mandy sat bolt upright and stared at Nina Terrance.

"Drummer, that's who you're imitating. Drummer. Phew. I was beginning to suspect that it was Drummer who said 'I got youv.' He's been acting strangely lately. Sort of quiet and scared. You aren't chasing him, are you?"

Mandy brushed the dirt off her pants and got to her knees. "Why am I getting so nervous? I guess 'cause I should have gotten Dad's help with you." She patted the bird. Nina throbbed her throat feathers, jabbed a leaf with her foot, and flew to her place on Mandy's shoulder.

"Ca! Ca! Ca! Ca!" Kray called from Trumpet Hammock. Nina Terrance crouched low and dug in her claws. Carefully Mandy pushed apart the long dry leaves and looked out across the woods toward the farm. She could see no one.

"Okay," she whispered, and Nina Terrance recovered from her fears, stood up, and roused.

"Caw!" called Kray. Mandy tucked Nina Terrance into her leaf nest, stroked her head, and whispered good-bye, then crept along the corridor of leaves to the palm tree door. Mandy suspected that Kray's alarm note had announced the presence of the hunters. She searched for her father and Jack.

After a zigzag hunt she wound up on the Trumpet Hammock side of Piney Woods. The sentinel on the stub was Kray; and Mandy knew by his pose that he was frightened. His head feathers were lifted, his wings were lowered, and his beak was open as he panted in fear. "The hunters,"

Mandy thought, for Kray's right eye was turned toward the strawberry field.

"Dad!" she called, running along the path under the rustling pines. In the field only mosquitoes and a few purple grackles moved. With a shrug she wandered on home, for the heat was oppressive and the sky was blackening over the banana patch.

Fred Tressel was coming out of the greenhouse as she opened the gate to the yard. His dirty hands bespoke the fact that he had been working there for a long time. She glanced back at Kray, who was now staring into the saw grass.

"A snake," she concluded and walked into the house.

7
The Reporters

Her guess seemed to be correct. The gun was back in the gun rack and Jack was at the typewriter laboriously thumping out a news story. Carver was on the telephone selling coupons and ads.

"Another *Waterway Times*?" she asked. "Is the SAAB busted?"

"No, we're making money for New York City," said Jack. "Dad's going to take us there after we've been to Cornell. Drummer wants to ride the subway, I'm signed up for a tour of *The New York Times*, and Carver wants to see a Broadway musical. So we need money."

"You sure do."

"Want to help?"

"I'm busy."

"Al Hathaway says there's a crazy crow at the village. It's trying to kill Barney."

"That would be nice for you."

Jack agreed and went on, "I think Al's making the crow up. I've been over there four or five times and haven't seen it. Want to check the story out?"

"I've got to do my homework."

"Aw, come on. Just run over there, please. Crows know we're hunters; but you're an innocent."

"Sorry." She washed out the lunch box, picked up her books and walked upstairs.

The next day Mandy hurried home from feeding Nina to see if the gun was in place. It was. Carver was pasting up ads, Jack was proofreading, and Fred was in the greenhouse. She had heard the "Ca! Ca! Ca! Ca!" alarm cry again, and yet everyone was here. No one had the gun. Owl or snake, she thought.

"Mandy," Jack bellowed. "Betty Howard says the crow slides down the sliding board."

"Impossible. Its feet would stick."

"Not this crow. She says it carries the lid of a coffee can to the top of the slide, steps in, and zip . . ." He plunged his hand toward the floor.

"Really?" Mandy covered her mouth with her hand. "Smart bird," she mumbled.

"Now will you check on it? I think Carv and I've killed too many crows for that bird to show for us."

"Send Drummer."

"I did. He always gets there too late. Come on, Mandy. Check it out for me, will you? I think this lady's a nut and

I don't want to be a fool and print a story only to find it's an aberration of her crazy old mind."

"Yeah," said Carver. "All we want you to do is go over there and watch the crow. Tell us if it's true . . . that's all. What a story if it is. We'd double our sales."

"If it's not and you print the story you'll lose your credibility?" Mandy asked teasingly.

"Exactly. Will you?" He poked her in the ribs.

"No." She put her elbows on the table and placed her brown chin in her hands. "You don't like what I write. What good is my word?"

Her lower lip was trembling—she could not control it. Carver felt sorry for her.

"I got you," he said. "Never mind. Eleven rejections makes us good for twelve."

Mandy straightened up. "Say that again, please."

"I mean it's okay. We've been lousy to you, why should you do us a favor?"

"No; say 'I got you' again."

"I got you. What's this?"

"It's not you," she said and walked into the living room leaving Jack and Carver baffled. They shrugged, decided it was too late for the crow story, and wrote up the village bus trip to the dog races instead.

Mandy flopped down on the couch, heard her mother's hair blower whining, and after crossing and uncrossing her feet as she tried to make up her mind to speak to her mother, finally gave in and went to her room.

"Mom," she said, sitting down on the bed. "Just how vindictive are crows?"

"What? Can't hear. Wait," she shouted over the motor whir.

Mandy watched her mother's brown hair prance in the gust, spiral, and fall softly to her neck. Finally she turned off the machine.

"You look worried, honey," Barbara said, reaching into her closet for a clean dress. "Anything wrong?"

"You said once that crows know about death and never forget people that hurt them. And that they almost seem to be vindictive and attack these people."

"Yes, I did say that. Doctor Bert has seen them punish and harass one of their own family members to vindicate some improper behavior known only to them."

Mandy blew a long breath from her lips. "We're all right then."

"What *are* you talking about?"

"Well, Nina Terrance has certainly seen everyone in this house, because she imitates me, Drummer, Dad, Jack, and Carv, and she hasn't attacked anyone . . . so I guess she is not vindictive."

"Maybe you're right. I surely hope so." Barbara studied her daughter. "You look as if you're harboring an awful truth. Do you know who killed Nina Terrance's parents?"

"Not for sure, Mommy," she answered. "But I know it isn't Carver. He just said 'I got you,' with no trembling slur on the 'you.'"

"So that leaves Dad and Jack."

"Yes," she said.

"Doctor Bert said that in another week or so the wild crows will lure Nina Terrance back to the forest and fields.

They don't like them to be pets of people, and they come and caw and talk to them when they are old enough to understand. The pet crow, seeing that it is a crow and not a human, takes off with its kinsmen."

"I'm all mixed up," said Mandy. "I want her to go and yet I like her so much, I want her to stay. It's so nice to have a friend. I even understand why Jack and Carver like to be so exclusive."

"Well, I hope they come for her soon. I'm not convinced she's entirely harmless. Being shot from a nest must leave a terrible imprint."

"But she's seen everyone and hasn't hurt a soul."

The warm trade wind blew through the window. Barbara smoothed her dress and viewed herself in the mirror. "I'm still curious about whose voice she imitates when she says, 'I got youv.' Maybe I'll come meet her."

"Oh, Mommy, yes." Mandy got up. "Tomorrow? Why don't we deliver the newspaper for the boys? They have a new edition coming out and none of them want to deliver them because of Barney."

"You think we can escape the dog?"

"Sure," said Mandy. "Yesterday when Barney growled at me Nina Terrance made him chase her and led him around the buildings until I went home. She teased him and kept him away from me."

"I want to see that." Barbara chuckled and tucked a handkerchief into her dress pocket. "By the way, Mrs. Howard wants you to come over and read to Meredith while she shops."

Mandy leaped from the bed and ran out of the room,

tomorrow's adventure spinning in her head. Tearing through the kitchen, she flipped Jack's hair as he thumped on the typewriter, and Drummer came in as she went out.

"The owls have owlets," he said, shutting the door firmly behind him after a glance at the trees. He darted to the sink and drank a large glass of water.

"What's the matter with you?" Mandy asked.

"Hot," replied Drummer and turned his back. She shrugged and hurried down the path to the woods, listening to the crows of Trumpet Hammock calling pleasantly to each other. Mandy stopped. These were new sounds. The guard crow had flown to Piney Woods and called five caws, and two crows in Trumpet Hammock had answered with three. They repeated their calls over and over. Mandy took the trail to Trumpet Hammock to watch what the crows did after getting these signals. They did nothing and Mandy concluded that the crows were using ordinary talk, sort of "I am fine. How are you?" By observing sound and effect she was learning their language.

"Ha, ha, ha, very funny," said Nina Terrance in Drummer's voice. Mandy looked up as the bird bent her wing tips up to ease her descent. She landed softly as a flower petal falling on Mandy's head.

They were in view of the house. Mandy ducked into the woods, then glanced back. Drummer was in the doorway staring in their direction.

"I hope he hasn't seen you," she said to Nina Terrance, who had moved to her shoulder. "Still, he's as loyal as a bee to a jasmine flower. He won't tell." Nina ran her beak down a strand of Mandy's hair as she would her own feather.

Mandy laughed and walked down the path toward Waterway Village.

"Drummer," she said to herself. "He's been so strange lately and now I know why. He knows I have a pet crow. He's keeping my secret, poor Drummer."

At the fork in the path that led off to Trumpet Hammock Mandy sat down and concentrated on yet another new signal she was hearing. "Cou-coi-ou," several crows were saying.

Presently a young crow flew out of the hammock with a feather in his beak. He dropped it as a companion came close behind. The second caught the feather and sped on, then he dropped it and the first bird spiraled downward and caught it.

"They're playing," exclaimed Mandy. "That new sound must mean 'Let's play feather ball or crow soccer' or something."

The grasses leaped and plunged near the log bridge and Drummer pushed out of the sedges and crossed to Trumpet Hammock. An iron stuck out of his backpack.

"The shotgun!" she gasped and focused narrowly. "Or is it?" Drummer pushed back the coco plum and disappeared into the forest.

Slowly, Mandy turned back. Nina Terrance dropped to the ground and walked beside her, stopping now and then to look at an insect. With a short flight and stab of her wedge-shaped beak she caught a beetle and ate it.

"Hey, none of that," said Mandy and picked her up. "I must feed you. None of this independence stuff."

"Kis, uk, ahh," Nina gabbled, instinctively using sounds

crows make when comfortable and secure in the roost, which was, in Nina's case, the top of Mandy's shoulder. Mandy smiled at her, then turned her thoughts to Drummer.

"That was a stick he had," she said aloud. "To kill snakes with. Wasn't it, Nina? You saw a stick, didn't you?"

"That's perfect!" yelled the bird and flew from her shoulder. Mandy laughed, but only halfheartedly; she was still trying to convince herself that what she had seen was a stick.

"That's perfect," Nina screamed again, then dropped to the ground and walked beside her like the doting child that she was. At the edge of the woods she took to her wings and, maneuvering them skillfully, soared, flapped, and slid to the fig tree. In the distance thunder rumbled as the fleecy clouds of afternoon piled into storm clouds.

Mandy knocked on Mrs. Howard's door just as the free village bus arrived to take the residents to the shopping mall. Meredith came running from the bedroom, pushed open the screen, and leaped into Mandy's arms. Mandy spun her around.

"Merry, how are you?" The little girl slid from her arms and ran indoors for her book. Hand in hand they walked to the sandbox and made themselves comfortable in the shade. The thunder sounded louder and closer. Mandy counted the time between lightning flash and thunder roll to gauge the arrival of the storm.

"It'll rain about sunset," she said to Meredith. "Time for lots of stories." As she opened the picture book, Mrs. Howard climbed on the bus and Mandy saw she was carrying the page of coupons from *The Waterway Times.* She was pleased. Tomorrow's issue had two pages of coupons, and she hoped she would sell every copy for her brothers.

That evening Mandy sat on her wide windowsill, arms wrapped around her knees, watching the crows of Trumpet Hammock file home in twos and threes. They were early and she wondered why—perhaps the hunting had been good. When all were in, the wind gusted across the saw grass. A thunderbolt exploded and the hammock disappeared behind a wall of rain. "They are weathermen, too," she said. "Wondrous birds."

Darkness and rain fell. "Now is the moment," she said, and placing her feet softly on the floor, she crossed to Drummer's room. She had to speak to him. His room was dark and empty and she remembered that he and Jack and Carver had gone off in the SAAB to get *The Waterway Times* from the young assistant printer who was working Sunday to get it done for his friends. She picked up one of Drummer's hand-drawn comic books, grinned, and began to read with pleasure.

Presently she heard the two-cycle engine of the SAAB about half a mile away, ringing and clinking as it rolled along sounding like a chain saw. She leaned out the window. The car came up the drive and stopped. Carver, Jack, and Drummer got out, hoisted *The Waterway Times* onto their shoulders, and, laughing and talking, came into the family room. She heard the TV sound out, the refrigerator door open and close, dishes tink, and finally feet thump as the boys walked around the dining room table collating the four pages of the newspaper.

At last Drummer's feet sounded on the steps, in the hall,

paused at his room, and came in. She stood up to meet him.

"Hey, what you doin' here?" he asked, then, not waiting for an answer, proudly held up *The Times* showing his drawing of Mr. Hathaway making a hole-in-one at the golf tournament.

"It's wonderful, Drummer," she exclaimed. "It looks just like him." Quickly she glanced through the paper checking on the news items. "I see they didn't mention the crow."

"I don't believe it's there," Drummer snapped and turned to his drawing board.

"You've never seen it?" she asked tentatively. "Crows aren't afraid of you. You should have." She studied his shoulders as he hunched over his paper and pen. Perhaps he wasn't keeping her secret after all. Perhaps he did not know she had a pet crow. Then why was he so remote these days?

Mandy decided to test Drummer's knowledge further.

"Well, I'm surprised you haven't seen her."

"Her?"

"Or him, who knows?" Flustered by her slip of the tongue, Mandy did not see Drummer nervously bite his thumbnail. "Guess you're just not around at the right times," she added.

"Guess not."

"Drummer, I saw you go into Trumpet Hammock today."

"The owl lives there."

"Were you carrying the shotgun? It's been missing lately."

"Me? I wish I had been. I'd love to be old enough to shoot."

"In the knapsack, Drummer? What did you have in the knapsack?"

"Me carrying a gun in the knapsack?" He laughed. "Come on, Mandy." He turned around and Mandy could see that his eyes were wide and innocent.

"Then it *was* a stick."

"I had the climbing irons in the knapsack. I climbed to the owl's nest."

"Oh, Drummer." She hugged him.

"What's the matter with you?" he asked, pulling away.

"Nothing. I just don't want you hurt."

"Hurt?" Drummer gave her a quick, frightened glance. "I'm not going to get hurt. I know all about the rules and Jack having to wait a whole year for sneaking the twenty-two rifle."

"Oh, that." Mandy realized she and Drummer were on different thought patterns, and she was relieved that his fears were only about possible punishment for taking the gun, not about a vindictive crow. She felt better. Stepping to the drawing board, she saw a pencil sketch of two owlets.

"Drummer, this is beautiful," she exclaimed.

"Got a poem to go with it?" he chided.

"I could almost write one," she said, touching the paper, in awe of her little brother's talent.

"You do write good, Mandy," he whispered. "And it would be nice to have you on the newspaper. Jack and Carver are getting old and businesslike. Dullsville. You and I could color up *The Times*, huh, Mandy?"

He was right, she thought and smiled down at him, then cleared her throat. "By the way, Drummer," she said, "when you get to New York would you do me a favor?"

"Sure, what?"

"I saw an ad in a magazine for a scarf. It's green and blue and has snowy egrets on it. They sell it at the gift shop at the Museum of Natural History."

"Hey, we're going there—I'll get it for you."

Mandy handed him an envelope of worn dollars and change from baby-sitting. "It'll look pretty with my blue dress," she said. Drummer put the money in the pocket of his good suit and went back to his table.

"How's Nina Terrance?" he asked as she turned to leave.

"She's fine. Wants to meet you someday."

"Yeah?" He bent over his work. "She's too fancy for me." Mandy laughed.

The next day Mandy raced home from the bus stop to find Barbara changing her clothes. She had taken off early to shop for the boys before they went to Ithaca, but primarily to deliver papers and meet Nina Terrance.

Drummer got a ride home in the SAAB with Jack and Carver. He ran into the house ahead of them, threw his books on the floor, and was headed for his room.

"Drummer," Jack said, "how about you delivering the papers today? I'm not going to fight off Barney again."

"If Dad'll let me take the gun and fill that dog with rock salt," he said, grinning.

"That'll be the day," Jack sneered. "Come on, Carver, it's your turn."

"How much would you pay me to deliver them?" Mandy piped.

"You?"

"Sure me."

"Barney'll rip you open."

"Barney never attacks me."

"How come?"

"I like animals; animals like me."

"Yeah? How about a dollar?"

"A dollar! No go."

"Two."

"Five! Or you do it yourself and get bit."

"Mom," protested Jack, "she's robbing us."

"Seems to me a whole leg is worth five dollars."

Jack saw he wasn't going to get any support from his mother and reluctantly agreed to Mandy's price. She lifted the canvas tote bag with the papers onto her shoulder and went to the door.

"Want to go, Mom?" she asked. "I'm going to meet Nina Terrance afterward. She wants to meet you."

"Well, okay," she said. "Barney likes me too. I'll go along." She picked up her purse and followed Mandy.

The three boys watched them swing down the path to the gate.

"Some gals we got," said Carver.

"What are we doing wrong?" said Jack, scratching his head.

Mandy and Barbara walked through Piney Woods in silence. Another afternoon storm of the rainy season was forming over Trumpet Hammock, the green-black clouds rumbling when split with shafts of lightning. Near the sable palm tree Mandy glanced back to see if she and her mother were being followed.

"Cak-ca," she called softly, and Nina Terrance walked out of the tent of huge leaves, saw Mandy, and flew to her shoulder.

"Nina, meet my mother," Mandy said. "Isn't she beautiful?"

"Ha, ha, ha. Very funny," Nina said in Drummer's voice. "Ha, ha, ha."

Barbara laughed in surprise and delight. "Mandy, she's marvelous! Just marvelous." Barbara held out her hand and the bird eyed her, sensed she played a gentle role in the human family, and stepped onto her wrist. There she cak-caed at Barbara and roused.

"That means she's comfortable with you," Mandy said as Nina's lifted feathers softened her head and body.

Barbara beamed at the crow. "Oh, I know Dad wouldn't mind this wonderful creature," she said. "We ought to bring her home."

"But maybe he shot her family, Mommy, and she'll attack him."

"That's true."

"On the path!" exclaimed Nina Terrance. "Ha, ha, ha. Very funny."

Barbara stroked the glossy black feathers and touched the throat layered with tiny feathers that vibrated when the bird spoke.

"She's extraordinary, Mandy," she whispered. "But you are exposing her to danger by keeping her a secret. Perhaps you should stop feeding her. She's still young enough to learn she's a crow. In a few more weeks it'll be too late."

Mandy sighed. "I agree . . . but not quite yet." She stroked Nina Terrance.

"Cak-ca," the bird said.

"Cak-ca," said Mandy.

At the edge of Waterway Village Nina Terrance flew from Barbara's hand and soared to the fig tree. Mandy searched for Barney. When he did not come out to meet them she was afraid the show of the year was not going to be.

"Ha, ha! ha!" Nina Terrance screamed, folded her wings against her body, and bulleted down the path around the trees to the edge of the woods.

"Very funny," she called. Barney barked from the back of Al Hathaway's house. Swooping down over the grass, the crow disappeared in the direction of the barking. Presently she reappeared, flying just out of reach of Barney. Snapping, leaping, howling, the dog chased her across the golf course and around the swimming pool. He did not even notice Barbara and Mandy knocking on the doors as they sold *The Waterway Times.*

Having purchased her copy, Mrs. Howard sat down on the chair on her porch to read the news and was waiting for Barbara and Mandy when they came by her apartment on their way home.

"How come that crow's not in the paper?" she asked.

"Carver and Jack still haven't seen her," Mandy explained. "As good reporters they only report what they see and can prove."

"They're crow hunters, you know," said Barbara, "and

crows are smart enough to keep out of sight of hunters. The crows of Trumpet Hammock actually know my husband and older sons. When they see them leave the house, they hide. This crow is hiding from them, too."

"The more I hear about crows," said Mrs. Howard, "the better I like them." Al Hathaway had come to Barney's rescue and was leading the exhausted dog home. Nina Terrance flew down from the tree. Barney saw her, wrenched himself from his master, and once more pursued the crow. With a caw of triumph, Nina Terrance led him around the golf course.

"I think it's time to exit," said Barbara.

They hastily told Mrs. Howard good night and hurried toward Piney Woods as Nina Terrance led Barney back to the swimming pool. When he almost had her tail in his teeth, she flew out over the water, and with a howl Barney leaped and plunged in.

Splashing and paddling, the dog floundered at the pool's edge until Mr. Hathaway rescued him. Nina, like an innocent sparrow, a guiltless bird on the wing, floated and soared, wings fully extended, tail ruddering, back to Piney Woods. She alighted quietly on the path and walked behind Mandy and Barbara to the sable palm, where Mandy picked her up, fed her, and returned her to her nest.

"Stay here," she said. "Tomorrow you get a prize for the best performer of the year. Cak-ca." She pressed her cheek to the warm feathers.

"Cak-ca," answered Nina Terrance and sat down.

When Mandy and Barbara came into the family room, Jack and Carver had the table set and were cooking hush puppies and ham. They turned as one and stared at the women as they put down the tote bag.

"Did you get chased?" Jack asked anxiously.

"Of course not," said Barbara.

Mandy poured the money out on the table, and counted out five dollars for herself.

"That may be the last issue of *The Waterway Times*," she said as she scooped up the change.

"Why?" Jack asked, startled.

"No crow story," she answered.

"Who wanted it?"

"Mrs. Howard."

"She's old and feeble." He turned his back. "That crow is in her head."

Drummer had been resting on the couch in the living room. He came to the kitchen to stare at Mandy and sidle close to his mother.

"You look pale, Drummer boy," Barbara said, slipping an arm around him. "Are you feeling all right?"

"Perfect," he snapped.

"Are you sure you should go tomorrow?"

"Yes," he said firmly.

She ran her hand over his forehead, decided he was all right, and picked up the teapot.

Fred Tressel came in the door, took off his muddy shoes, and peered into the frying pan at the cornmeal hush puppies.

"Let's eat and get to bed," he said. "Everybody's got to be up by four-thirty tomorrow to catch the plane to New York."

8
The Tapping

Mandy was awakened the next morning by the taxi honking. She crawled out of bed and came downstairs to remind Drummer about the scarf. If he had looked ill last night, he seemed radiantly healthy this morning as he ran out the door. Glancing up at the trees, he dove into the cab.

Her father hugged her warmly.

"I wish you were coming, too," he said. "Next time it's just you and Mom and me." Sleepily Mandy kissed his rough cheek, laughed to see him in a business suit, and took her mother's hand as the cab drove off into the morning mist.

The wood storks screamed their primitive calls from their roost in the Glades, the backyard mockingbird sang to the dawn, and Kray announced the rising of the sun. The air was warm and moist even though the night was not entirely pushed back. Mandy and Barbara looked at each other and went back to their beds.

Around seven o'clock Mandy heard the crow clan cawing, and coming awake realized they were not at Trumpet Hammock but very close by. She threw open the screen and looked out. There on the strawberry table sat Nina Terrance, and yelling at her from the top of the orange tree were Kray and two scouts.

Mandy dressed as she ran down the stairs.

"Mom! Look out the window," she called.

Barbara Tressel was enjoying a second sleep in the quiet house. She mumbled as Mandy burst into her room.

"There are crows in our yard!"

"Crows?" she said, coming awake completely. "I've *never* seen crows in our yard."

She flung on her bathrobe and stepped to the window.

"Good lord!" she exclaimed. "This is the first time I've ever seen crows here. They must know the men are gone."

"How do they know they're not off to the store and coming right back?" asked Mandy incredulously.

"I don't know," replied Barbara, shivering at their insight. "I really don't know."

Mandy pointed to Kray. Like all leaders in the animal world, he held his head higher than the others, appeared larger and more regal. His pose was one of relaxed confidence.

"That's Kray," Mandy said. "See the crease in his head feathers?"

"Now I see why he hates the Tressel men. He had a narrow escape."

Two more crows arrived from Trumpet Hammock and yelled at Nina Terrance.

"What are we going to do?" asked Barbara. "The bananas are ripening. Your father will be furious if they are harmed. Shall I show them the gun?"

"They only seem interested in Nina Terrance. Wait a minute."

Kray tilted his head, then thumped the feathers of his throat and called out a clarion "Caaaw, caaaw, caaaw, caaaw," the assembly call which usually meant "Come harass the owl." Now it meant "Gather 'round the errant crow." One by one the crows of Trumpet Hammock appeared in the sky, winged over the strawberry field, and dropped down onto the fig tree. They arranged themselves about the limbs, staring down at Nina.

"Why, they've come to take Nina Terrance," exclaimed Barbara. "Just like Doctor Bert said."

"Oh, Mommy. I don't want them to. I've changed my mind."

"It's best, Mandy. She'll survive if she goes now."

"Oh, Mommy." Mandy's voice was almost inaudible. "Not yet."

Nina Terrance looked curiously at her kinsmen, blinked her feather-rimmed eyes, and flew down on the path. Sauntering from side to side in the manner of the ground-walking crow, she strode up the path to the steps. With three hops she took care of the steps and arrived at the door.

TAP. TAP. TAP. Nina Terrance struck her beak against the wooden frame. Mandy stared at her mother and her mother stared back. "Caaaw, caaaw, caaaw, caaaw," arose in frantic cacophony from the crows of Trumpet Hammock as they reprimanded the errant crow.

Nina rapped harder.

"She's knocking to get in," said Mandy.

"So it seems."

"Shall I let her in?"

"Maybe not."

"Why?"

"This may be the decision point. If you, her mother, do *not* appear, she may leave with the crows."

"Nonsense," said Mandy. "The crows are giving the harassment get-the-owl cry, not the you-are-one-of-us cry."

"Wild crows get upset when they see pet crows," said Barbara. "They are trying to call her back to them."

"They'll kill her like they kill little owlets," Mandy said. She ran out of the bedroom and sprinted through the kitchen to the door. Kray had flown closer to Nina Terrance and was now screaming without letup. Nina circled the step indecisively, walking first toward Kray and then toward the house. The sound of Mandy's footsteps caused her to pause. On the other side of the screen Mandy held the doorknob, wondering what to do. Kray was now coaxing warmly, softly. "Car-r-a-ck." Nina seemed curiously interested.

Mandy opened the door. Nina Terrance, upon seeing her mother, walked in.

"Nevah, nevah!" screamed Kray in distress.

"Ha, ha, ha. Very funny. Ha, ha, ha," said Nina Terrance and flew onto the table.

"Mandy!" Barbara was standing in the kitchen doorway.

"Just this once, Mommy. Then I'll never feed her again."

"Perfect," yelled Nina.

Barbara covered her mouth and laughed despite her concern. "She really *is* a person," she said. "I have this awful feeling that I shouldn't laugh or I'll offend her."

The table had been set last night for Mandy and Barbara's first breakfast alone. Nina Terrance looked it over, eyed a silver fork, picked it up, and dropped it. She tapped a glass and pecked the flower on the paper napkin. Then she stabbed a spoon.

"She likes shiny things," said Mandy, putting down a plate for Nina. The bird fluttered and begged like a nestling, and Mandy fed her leftover hush puppies.

"Caw, ah!" called Kray, giving the come-get-the-food signal. He was perched on a vine just above the window, where by leaning down he could look into the house. When he straightened up, the people in the house could not see him.

"Caw, ah," he repeated. Two crows joined him, cocked their heads, and peered down into the family room. Mandy saw them fly to the tree, but when she glanced up they sat tall and vanished.

"Caaaw, caaaw, caaaw, caaaw"—"Assemble."

Down from the trees, in from the Glades, came the crows of Trumpet Hammock. By ones and twos they settled on limbs and lawn. With concern, Barbara watched them gather.

"I think I had better scramble a dozen eggs," she said. "If I feed the crows until they are stuffed maybe they'll leave the bananas alone."

When Mandy went to the refrigerator for orange juice, Nina Terrance dropped to the floor and walked quietly behind her, waited until she had opened the door, and flew to the meat shelf. She landed on the ham, turned, and fluttered her wings to be fed.

"Caw, ah," yelled one of the scouts at Kray's side.

Up from the lawn came the other crows. They alighted on the hibiscus bush, the vine, and the rainspout and stared down through the window at the food in the refrigerator, garbling soft sounds of "crow heaven."

"They're so friendly," Mandy said. "Really, Daddy and the guys just shouldn't shoot crows. They're worth more than all the old berries they could eat."

"Open the back door," said Barbara, carrying the heavy frying pan across the room. On the back steps she noted Kray's royal appearance, his confidence and dignity.

"Where do you wish to be served, Sir Kray?" she asked. Kray cocked an eye and pulled in his feathers momentarily, sizing up the big black pan. He sensed it would not explode, and relaxed.

"Would you like it here on the lawn?" she went on, although Kray had put a clump of leaves between them and she could not see him. Soft caws sounded among the leaves as the crows discussed the food on the ground. The guard of the hour flew down and ate a bite. Kray focused sharply on the bird. Minutes passed and he did not drop dead from some poison.

"Caw, ah," announced Kray.

"Maybe that's a terrible thing to do," Barbara said. "They'll come back and get shot."

"They're too smart for that."

Kray dropped out of the tree and, holding his head high,

walked gingerly among the bits of egg. Cocking his eye toward the house, he suddenly stabbed and gobbled. Down from the leaves and limbs came the rest of the clan, and within minutes the eggs were gone. Mandy tossed out some bread.

"We're *really* asking for trouble," said Barbara, but she smiled as she stirred up another batch of eggs for herself and Mandy. With the rising of the sun she had been transported into a new world where the people wore feathers and wings.

Barbara and Mandy sat down to their breakfast in thoughtful silence, unaware of Nina Terrance, who was pulling the ribbon out of Jack's typewriter. Having demolished it, she flew to the table.

"Welcome to our home, Nina Terrance," said Barbara to the crow. "I'm so glad you were able to come." ·

"How are your braces?" Mandy asked.

The bird cocked an eye at her, then begged for food, fluttering her wings and opening her beak. Mandy fed her.

"You *do* have a baby," said Barbara. "The young crows outside are eating on their own. Nina Terrance will never become independent and leave home if you keep making such an infant of her."

"That's the kind of child I want, Mrs. Tressel," said Mandy. "I never want her to leave home."

"I suppose you're right. I have a daughter too. And I never want *her* to leave home."

"Good," Mandy blurted so loudly she scared Nina Terrance. She flung out her wing, knocking over Mandy's milk glass, and it smashed with a tinkle. Mandy jumped up from the table.

"Except at times like this," added Barbara, pushing back her chair and hurrying to the sink for the dishcloth.

Another strong tap sounded. Kray was at the door.

"He's copying Nina Terrance," said Barbara. "Guess he feels that if she can get toast, marmalade, and eggs, so can he."

"Shall we invite him in?"

"Why not? We've gone this far," replied Barbara.

Kray stood on the top step, neck stretched up, feathers pressed tightly to his body. Barbara opened the screen door. He eyed her perceptively, then the room, the table, the food. Giving Mandy a quick glance, he walked through the door toward Nina Terrance. She dropped to the floor and threatened this intruder by erecting her feathers. Kray flew above her and sat on the table.

"CAW," he said, meaning "All's well" this time. But Nina Terrance, seeing his dark form above her head, screamed: "I got youv!" She ran under the table.

"That voice," gasped Barbara. "Whose is it?" But her words died on her tongue.

Kray, hearing the killer's voice, flew for the window, struck the screen, and fell to the floor.

"Ca! Ca! Ca! Ca!" he cried. Instantly the crows outside spread their wings and, in silence, flapped over the yard and the strawberry field and vanished into Trumpet Hammock.

When Kray recovered his composure, he took to his wings, knocked over a vase, crashed into the TV antenna, and flying past the bookcase, scattered *The Waterway Times* like leaves in the wind.

Nina Terrance stayed under the table watching. Although

she envisioned herself as a person, the terror in this creature triggered her inherited instincts.

"Ca! Ca! Ca! Ca!" she called in weak imitation of the alarm cry. Kray slammed himself against another window.

"Mommy, what shall we do?"

"Get a dish towel. Scare him toward the door." Barbara flung it open, but Kray was confused. He circled the room higher and higher, and then panting, beak open, he struck the ceiling.

"Car-r-a-ck," Mandy clucked. Kray heard the lovesick note of the crow and dropped to the table. He tilted his head and curiously eyed the girl.

"Cak-ca, cak-ca," said Nina Terrance from under the table, but only Mandy understood. Kray folded his wings, dropped to the floor, and with a conversational "Caw, caw, caw" strode toward the door, head held jauntily high. Fright comes and goes quickly in birds, as do feelings of aggression and anger. He glanced around the room, saw the open door, and spreading his wings, soared directly through it. Crossing the yard, he flew in a perfectly straight line to Trumpet Hammock.

"As the crow flies," said Barbara and flopped down in the armchair. "Good heavens," she added. "I have witnessed an event."

"I'm sorry, Mommy." Mandy swept up the broken glass and shattered vase. "I'm really sorry."

"Don't be. We have been fortunate. We have been witnesses to a conversation between people and crows."

"What do you mean?"

"Well, whoever imprinted 'I got youv' on Nina Terrance is someone Kray knows. He just told us how much he feared the person."

"Did it sound like Daddy?"

"A little, but not really. Too high-pitched. And the 'youv'—he doesn't lisp." Barbara brushed back her hair and slowly got to her feet. She picked up the scattered pages of *The Times.* Mandy straightened the TV antenna and Nina Terrance hopped upon the broom and then on the back of the chair.

"There's a good program on TV pretty soon," said Mandy. "Is it okay if Nina Terrance stays to see it?"

"I'd be charmed to have her, but don't you think you ought to give her mother a ring and let her know she'll be late."

Mandy, always happy when her mother entered her fantasy world, flung her arms around her.

A sucking snap sounded. She turned to see Nina Terrance on the table by the refrigerator door, prying it with her beak. The door swung open; she flew in and alighted on the butter.

Mandy looked up at her mother. "Clever, isn't she?"

"But rude," said Barbara. "She must be taught some manners."

The refrigerator door, designed to close on its own, began to move.

"Careful," Barbara gasped. So keen was Nina Terrance's sense of disaster, however, that she flew off with the butter in her beak before the door slammed shut.

"This is going to be a very eventful vacation," said Barbara, sitting down.

"What do you mean 'going to be'?" said Mandy, chasing Nina and the butter around the room.

9
Nina Speaks Crow

Over the rumble of dawn's fading storm Mandy heard someone tapping on her window. She rolled to her belly. Nina Terrance was on the sill peering in. When she saw Mandy's eyes she rapped again, her meaning perfectly clear. Unnerved by the bird's knocking, Mandy slipped out of bed and threw up the screen.

"What do you want?" she asked, knowing full well the bird had already said she wanted to come in.

"Cak-ca," said the crow and stepped over the sill, looked around the room, and rousing her feathers, shook them lightly to say she was at ease.

"Thank you. I'm glad you like my nest," replied Mandy.

Nina Terrance flew to the floor, pecked the rug fringe, and then hop-winged to the straight-back chair. With a jump she alighted on the desk and picked up a pencil.

"Hey, if *you* write a story for *The Waterway Times* I know Jack will print it," Mandy said. " 'Crow Interviews Girl,' *that's* news!"

Mandy opened her bureau drawer to take out clean clothes. Nina Terrance flew into the drawer, tossed out a pair of socks, stabbed at the T-shirts, and taking a scarf in her beak, trailed it to the top of the bureau. There she dropped it and walked over the hairbrush and a book to the mirror. She peered at the bird in the reflection. Mandy waited to see if she would be frightened or friendly.

Nina Terrance gave the image a quick glance, saw Mandy in the reflection, and reacted by fluttering and begging Mandy's image.

"You can't see yourself," she said. "You must still think you look like me." She smiled. As long as Nina thought she was a person, the crows could not lure her away.

Having acknowledged her mother, Nina Terrance stepped to a box, picked out a ring, put it down, flipped a silver chain into the air, and pecked a bracelet. Then she flew back to the floor. Pecking the design on the rug, the cracks in the wood, she wandered under the bed. Mandy, seeing that she had not yet made it, pulled up the bedspread, then flung herself on the bed to straighten the far side.

"Here comes that damn dog again!" screamed Nina Terrance, running out from under the dark plunging mass. Swiftly she flew to the window.

"Cak-ca, cak-ca," said Mandy softly. The dark moving bed overhead had affected Nina as if it had been a hawk.

"Cak-ca," answered Nina Terrance and flew to Mandy's

shoulder. Mandy soothed the bird with sounds and strokings.

Downstairs in the kitchen Nina winged to the table beside the refrigerator, pried it open and peered in. With a pounce she landed on the strawberry shortcake.

"Dessert you get," said Mandy, carrying platter, cake, and Nina Terrance to the table, where she broke her off a bite. The crow swallowed, blinked, and begged furiously for more.

When all but a small chunk was devoured, Nina Terrance sat down, keeping herself from toppling by spreading her wings. "Ca," she said faintly and refused the last bite.

"Let's take Mom a cup of coffee," Mandy said, pouring boiling water over instant coffee. Nina was too full to stir, so Mandy put her on the tray with the cup and saucer and went to the bedroom.

"Cak-ca," she said to her mother.

"I'm dreaming," Barbara said and pushed herself up to a sitting position. "Breakfast in bed served by a beautiful young girl and a crow who is really a prince in disguise."

"Ha, ha, ha. Very funny. Ha, ha, ha," screamed Nina Terrance, and Barbara laughed so heartily that she frightened the crow. She flew to the dresser top.

"That's perfect," said Nina Terrance, picking up a button.

"Oh, Mommy. I wish Daddy could see her. He'd never shoot crows again."

"At least not her."

Nina Terrance screamed, "Ha, ha, ha," then became utterly silent. Barbara's dresser top was a veritable treasure house of shiny objects, and Nina stretched up her neck. She had landed in crow heaven. She picked up a ring, then a watch. Next she pecked the glittering hand mirror and, spying an earring of blue glass, hopped upon it with a caw of excitement.

"Give me that," said Barbara, but Nina Terrance had put it under her tongue.

"Ca-rak," the bird answered, lifting the hairlike vibrissae near her nostrils. .

"What does that mean?" asked Barbara.

"That she is about to be playfully bad. She says that when she opens the lunch box and steals food."

"Is she going to steal my earring?"

"Going to? I think she already has." Mandy laughed. "Try to get it back." Barbara took hold of Nina's beak, but no prying could open it.

"Oh, well, she can have it," said Barbara. Nina Terrance, not waiting for consent, had flown to the floor. Sneaking in a crouch, she went around the chair and out the door. Mandy and Barbara followed her down the hall, through the kitchen, to the back door. She knocked strongly.

"Are you sure she can have it?" asked Mandy. "You may never see it again."

"Not much choice." Barbara smiled. "So let's see what she does with it."

When Mandy opened the door Nina Terrance flew into the woman's-tongue tree. Searching the limbs, she hopped amid the branches until she came to a large crotch. As wind tossed the long dry pods, they clattered and murmured like voices and swayed like a dancing screen, while Nina Terrance hid her blue earring in the crotch and pounded it. After checking for spies she flew back to the door and knocked, and Mandy let her in.

"The eggs are ready," Mandy said to the crow, who daintily put down first one foot and then the other as she sashayed, then flew, to the tabletop. There she eyed the plates. When she saw the biscuits, bacon, and eggs she begged for food, although not hungry. Mandy offered her a sip of orange juice, which she gargled and spit out; then she begged again.

"I thought you were going to stop feeding her, Mandy," Barbara said.

"I'm all mixed up about her, Mommy. Sometimes I want her to go so she'll be safe; but then I think maybe nobody in our house will see her and I can keep her forever."

"But suppose she tries to get even with whoever did the shooting?"

"Then I'll stop feeding her."

"That might be too late. The crows won't be able to reeducate her after a certain time."

"She'll learn."

"But the young crows of Trumpet Hammock are being driven off now, off to set up new homes and new families many miles away."

"So?"

"She has to go with them or not at all. If she passes up the moment to disperse she'll remain here, a threat and threatened."

"Do all animals do that?" Mandy asked, changing the subject.

"As far as I know. The higher animals do. Leaving home prevents interbreeding and the weakening of the gene pool."

"Do people disperse?"

"Of course. Your daddy and I moved away from our homes in Everglades City. You and the boys will go out from here to make your homes."

"It sounds scary."

"That's because you're not ready to go. When the time comes, you'll be eager."

Nina Terrance had flown to the floor and was now knocking on the door.

Mandy let her out, smiling as she watched her pause on the top step and preen her feathers. "Ha, ha, ha," the bird said.

"CAW, CAW," said Kray conversationally from the guard post on Trumpet Hammock.

"CAW," answered Nina Terrance lifting her wings. "CAW." She hesitated. "Ca," she murmured with a lack of confidence.

"Mommy," Mandy exclaimed. "She's talking crow talk!"

Barbara arose and, standing behind Mandy, looked down on the bird. "This is good," she said. "It's not too late for her to return. Let her go!"

"CAW, CAW," said Nina Terrance, cocking her head in Kray's direction.

"CAW, CAW, CAW," answered the leader of the crows.

Nina Terrance walked down the steps, hopped along the path to the gate, then flew off toward Trumpet Hammock.

"Now, for heaven's sake, Mandy," said Barbara. "Don't feed her anymore. Here's your chance."

"Caw," called Nina Terrance from the distance.

"Cak-ca," yelled Mandy. She glanced at her mother to see if she knew what she had said to the crow. Apparently she did not, for the next thing she said was: "Good girl. Tell her to go."

10
The Shopping Center

When Nina Terrance rapped on the window the next morning Mandy hesitated, then let her in. She did not go downstairs right away, however. Instead she put new laces in her sneakers, read, and finally, when she heard Barbara start the car, wandered down to the kitchen with Nina Terrance. After feeding her, she let her outside. The crow flew to the woman's-tongue tree and, creeping up the limbs, found her blue earring. Mandy sat on the step, arms around her knees, watching the bird flip the dangly jewelry over her head and under her wing.

"When Daddy comes home," she said to Nina, "everything will be all right. I'm going to tell him what I did. He'll understand. I'll promise to keep you out of the strawberries. I love you so."

When Saturday morning arrived Mandy knew Barbara

would be home all day, so she got up before the crows and carried breakfast to the woods.

Pushing back the leaves of the sable palm, she crawled to Nina Terrance and awoke her. Ever since Mrs. Howard had said that Nina had slept in the fig tree, she had put her to bed in the palm herself.

"Here, Nina, now it's your turn for breakfast in bed." She sat down in the cool shadows. "Today, I am going to study you for science," she said to appease her feeling of guilt for feeding Nina after her conversations with her mother. "I will find out where you go during the day and give my notes to Doctor Bert for his publications."

"Cak-ca," said the crow, then walked to the opening in the old leaves and peered out at the dewy morning. She preened, cleaned her toes, polished her beak, then flew to a bush. Mandy followed her. A wildness came to Nina's eyes and she spread her wings and flew to the gumbo-limbo tree that grew just off the path by the strawberry field. She sidestepped along a limb to a hollow, peered in, and quivered the vibrissae around her nostrils. "Ca-rak," said Nina in her private language.

"You're feeling impish again," said Mandy and wrote that down in her notebook. Nina Terrance reached into the hole and picked out a bright new quarter that gleamed in the sun as she held it over her head. Putting it under her toes, she pounded it with her beak, then replaced it in the hollow. Next she took out a dime.

"Money, *wow!*" exclaimed Mandy. "Now we're really in trouble. You've been stealing. Someone might shoot you for that." Mandy crossed her arms and rubbed her shoulders as she thought what to do. Although the bird had no concept of stealing, Mandy was well aware that animals that live with man must abide by man's moral code. A dog must not bite, a cat must not kill birds, and a crow, for heaven's sake, must not steal money.

Nina Terrance returned her dime to the hollow, winged to a low tree limb, and flew down to the path. She walked along ca-rakking at a beetle, then a spider on its dewy web, at a toad and a green anolis lizard. Occasionally she tossed a leaf in the air and watched it flutter and fall.

At the edge of the forest she peered across the golf course. The morning sun was still low enough to be comfortable, and the residents of Waterway Village were outdoors playing golf or sitting in the sun before the bugs and heat of midmorning drove them inside.

Although Meredith had gone home, her shovels and buckets were still in the sandbox neatly lined up, waiting for her return. Nina flew over the box, tilted her eye to focus on a spoon, then alighted on the fig tree. She preened and wiped her beak while watching the golfers.

Presently she soared out over the green and landed near Mr. and Mrs. Colman, retired schoolteachers who now taught a course in banking to their neighbors.

"Here's that crow, Morris," Mrs. Colman said. He turned around, saw Nina Terrance walking behind him, and with a grin reached into his pocket.

"I know what you want, you old beggar," he said and tossed her a dime. She caught it in her beak.

"Hey! That's a new trick," he exclaimed and pulled out

another coin. He tossed it to her and she caught this one, too.

When Betty Howard came out to sun on her porch, Mr. Colman called to her.

"Come see this circus crow," he said. Mrs. Howard limped across the greens, glancing at the clouds that were beginning to darken and threaten rain.

"What's up?" she said. "Does that crow dance?"

Mr. Colman tossed a quarter. Nina caught it and put it under her tongue with the dime and nickel.

"Now that's news," exclaimed Betty Howard. "Why don't those Tressel boys write about this crow . . . even if they don't see her? We do."

Another golfer joined them and marveled at the clever bird, and she too threw Nina Terrance a coin. When Nina had all she could carry, she abandoned two of the dimes and flew off for the woods, flying low under the weight of her treasures.

"Seems to know his limit," observed Mr. Colman. "One dime more and he wouldn't be able to fly. Wonder if he's aware of that?"

"I'm sure she is," said Mrs. Howard. "She's smarter than most people."

"She *is* smart," said Mrs. Colman. "She's getting rich off us. She should be teaching the banking course."

Nina Terrance sailed through the woods just above the path, rounding the bends with tilts and scoops of her wings, and Mandy, running full out, followed her to the gumbo-limbo tree. There Nina placed a few of the coins in the hollow, found a loose piece of bark under which she stuffed a quarter, and placed the last dime in a nearby tree. Then, glancing around for spies, she flew back to the sable palm tree, where Mandy caught up with her a few minutes later.

Seeing Mandy, Nina Terrance crouched and begged. Mandy reached into her pocket and pulled out fish and cooked carrots wrapped in aluminum foil. Nina gobbled and begged.

"No more," she scolded. The bird cried pitifully and Mandy took a cookie out of another pocket.

"Now hush up," she said, tapping the bird's shiny beak in a fond reprimand. Backing out of the shelter, Mandy ran home to recopy her notes.

Halfway through lunch with her mother, Mandy heard Nina Terrance rap on the door. She got up to let her in.

"Don't give her anything to eat," Barbara said when the crow came to the table and begged.

"Okay." Upon hearing her mother's signal to relax, Nina sat down on her empty plate and tucked her beak under the feathers on her back. Slowly her eyes closed, the lids coming up from the bottom, not down from the top as do the eyelids of mammals.

"I miss Daddy," said Mandy, "but I guess it's just as well he's not here. Nina won't come to meals with us when he and the other hunters are home."

"I hope by then she won't want to," said Barbara.

Nina Terrance awoke, yawned, and flew to the door. Mandy let her out. On the top step she extended her neck and stretched a leg and wing on one side and then the other.

With a head jerk she glanced at the coconut palm in the yard. A movement had caught her eye.

"Caaaw, caaaw, caaaw, caaaw." Four crows screamed the assembly call in unison. Three others came winging across the Glades to the edge of the yard. They also caaawed to assemble. One of these was Kray. Nina Terrance cocked her head and listened, then walked in a circle, uninterested. They flew to the woman's-tongue tree, Kray in the lead, and all called to the strange crow that had a little girl for a mother. Their cries rose to a frantic pitch.

"They're really trying to convince her today," said Barbara. "I hope she is getting the idea that she *is* a crow."

Nina Terrance hopped down a step, walked to its edge, and jumped down to the next one. The crow talk became more urgent as she came toward them. They were winning. Tilting her head, focusing on Kray, Nina Terrance began to blink. She was seeing the crows as her look-alikes for the first time. She hopped down another step.

"Cak-ca, cak-ca." Mandy rolled their love call softly from the back of her throat.

"Cak-ca," replied Nina Terrance. She roused, looked up, and flew to her shoulder.

"Hey, did you call her back?" Barbara asked. "She seemed to be leaving. Then you sort of rattled and she stopped."

"I just told her I liked her," said Mandy.

"No food?"

"No, I have no food."

"I thought she was programmed to food . . . but there seems to be more to a baby crow than its belly."

Mandy rubbed her cheek against the warm dusty feathers and listened to Nina mumble "Cak-ca" as she ran her beak down the threads of Mandy's hair.

"Caw, caw, caw." Kray spoke, flying to the vine above the window.

"CAW," answered Nina with such force that she startled herself. "Ha, ha, ha. Very funny." The instincts within the bird programmed her to return, and once more she turned toward Kray.

"Ca! Ca! Ca! Ca!" he exploded. Like a storm of black rain, the crows of Trumpet Hammock dropped down from the trees, opened their wings, and sailed, as if driven by hurricane winds, to the cover of the hardwood forest.

Nina Terrance dug in her claws and crouched, unable to move.

"What scared Kray?" Barbara gasped in astonishment. "There's no one here but us crow lovers. No hawks flew overhead, no owls . . ."

Mandy cradled Nina Terrance in her hands and went inside. She looked at the vine where Kray had sat, then to the other side of the room.

"The guns!" she exclaimed. "Mommy, he saw the guns. He knows what they are even without a person holding them."

Barbara, cupping her hands around her face as if to see better, stepped inside.

"The guns, of course," she said, and lifted one from the rack.

"I got youv," screamed Nina Terrance.

"Whose voice is that?" Barbara asked.

"Maria's?" said Mandy. "It's high-pitched and tense . . . like Maria's voice. But she doesn't shoot."

"Yes, she does. She shot pigeons for her family in Puerto Rico."

"Mommy, call her up and ask her if she shot the crows' nest."

"I'll see her this afternoon. She's coming over to help thin the strawberry seedlings."

"I hope so. I hope she shot the nest. If she did, then Nina won't attack anyone in the family. I'll tell Maria and she'll stay away and Daddy will let me keep Nina Terrance."

"Where are you going?" Barbara asked as Mandy followed the crow to the garden gate.

"I'm following her. Taking notes on her," she called, "for Doctor Bert."

Mandy waved to her mother and ran after Nina Terrance, who had flown to the edge of Piney Woods. When she caught up with her she was sitting in her lookout tree near Waterway Village. Unaware of Mandy now, she sailed out across the golf course, across the hedge of Australian pines, and out over the road. The last Mandy saw of her she was beating her wings in the direction of the shopping center. She started to chase her across the golf course when Betty Howard came out of her apartment with her handbag and cane and walked toward the village bus parked at the end of her path.

"Are you going to the shopping mall?" Mandy called.

"Yes, to the Halle's Corner Mall."

"Can I hitch a ride?"

"Come along."

As Mandy took a seat beside Mrs. Howard, the bus pulled forward a few doors and Mr. Hathaway came aboard with Barney on a leash.

"He's taken to giving that dog an outing in the shopping mall ever since the crow has been trying to kill him," Mrs. Howard said. Mandy felt a small twinge of conscience until she recalled the rip in Jack's pants. Barney snarled and curled up at Mr. Hathaway's feet.

The bus drove down an avenue of royal palm trees to the shopping mall, a complex of low buildings designed to resemble a Seminole Indian village with fake thatched roofs and pine posts. Mandy was searching the palms in the parking lot for Nina Terrance when she saw a large crowd of people gathered around the hardware store. "Coupons," she thought as she walked toward them. "Jack and Carver are doing okay for Pete Moore." Then she saw Nina Terrance standing on top of a sliding board on display outside the store with a box top in her beak. Mandy pushed her way into the crowd.

"What's going on?" she asked an elderly man in T-shirt, shorts, and sneakers.

"That crow," he said. "Watch him. He puts that box top down, steps on it, and slides down the board. He's a scream. Someone called the Eyewitness News at the TV station and the reporters are here to film him." The man chuckled. "Funniest crow I ever saw."

Mandy stepped near the cameras to watch. Nina Terrance flew to the top of the slide, put down the box top, stepped onto it, and slid to the bottom. The cameras rolled and the people cheered. As Nina picked up her box top and flew back to the top of the slide, Mandy tapped the reporter's shoulder.

"That crow can speak English," she said. Maybe Mandy could not write a news story, but she was going to make sure her pet made headlines. "Ha, Jack," she said to herself.

The camera was on Mandy. The reporter was nudging her. She smiled and looked up.

"Did you say this crow talks?"

"Yes," replied Mandy.

"How can we make her talk?"

Mandy pointed to Alvin Hathaway, who stood at the edge of the crowd with Barney on the leash.

"Ask Mr. Hathaway to let his dog go," she said, "and the crow will talk."

The reporter hurried to Alvin Hathaway and asked if he would release his dog. Pleased to have his beloved Barney and himself on television, he unsnapped the leash and Barney bounded forward.

"Get your camera on the crow," said Mandy to the cameraman. "She's going to talk."

"Here comes that damn dog again!" yelled Nina Terrance, her throat pulsating, her beak open. Then she put down the box top, slid down the slide, and sailed off on her wings at the bottom. She flew low around the people and positioned herself above Barney's nose. He leaped, bellowed, and springing into the air, chased the irritating crow in and out among the cars, people, and palms. Finally she returned to the top of the slide and Barney collapsed on the ground.

Mandy decided she had better leave before she was asked for her name and address. If she was going to keep Nina

Terrance, she wanted to tell her dad before he learned about Nina from the townspeople. While the newsman and cameraman filmed the crow and dog, Mandy slipped inside the hardware store and watched from behind a display of nails.

"The show's not over," store owner Pete Moore announced after stepping outside. "Watch this." The camera swung around as Pete held up a fifty-cent piece. Nina eyed it, flew above his head, and took the coin in her beak. She carried it back to the slide. There she flipped and played with it, put it under her tongue, and looking into the camera, said: "Ha, ha, ha. Very funny!" The people laughed uproariously.

"She gets paid for her act," shouted Pete, posing for the camera beside the name of his store. Suddenly Nina took off and soared up over the building and out of sight. Mandy slipped out of the back of the hardware store and found Betty Howard in the grocery store.

"I'm going to walk home," she said. "Don't wait for me."

"Wasn't our crow wonderful?" Betty said. "I can't wait to see her on the TV tonight." She hobbled closer to Mandy. "That crow must have a fortune by now. This man's been giving her money for a week or more. He told me it was good advertisement."

Mandy slipped out the back door and ran most of the way to Piney Woods. She found Nina Terrance in the gumbo-limbo tree and sat down to see what came next in the extraordinary life of Nina Terrance. She simply preened and behaved like a contented crow for the next hour.

Around four o'clock Mandy remembered that Maria would be at the farm and got to her feet.

"Cak-ca," said Nina when she saw Mandy was moving, and alighted on her head, then her shoulder.

Mandy walked to the far side of Piney Woods and sat down to contemplate. Maria was in the field taking up the plastic weed inhibitors. If she was the culprit, Nina Terrance would surely attack her now. Mandy glanced at the bird on her shoulder. She was calmly lifting a strand of Mandy's hair. No luck. Mandy got up and crossed the field to say hello to Maria. After a few yards Nina Terrance spread her wings and flew back to the forest.

"Could be she's afraid of her," said Mandy to herself, "but not very." She decided to go give Nina the final test and walked close to Maria.

"Como va, Mandy Tressel?" said Maria warmly, and Mandy fairly cried as she realized it could not possibly be Maria. She didn't speak English!

"A crow's right behind you," gasped Maria in Spanish. "I've never seen a crow in this field. Your father will be angry." Mandy, who was studying Spanish in school, understood her well enough.

"Shoo!" Maria plunged toward the crow, who lifted her wings and flew to Mandy's shoulder.

"Ha, ha, ha. Very funny. Ha, ha, ha," said Nina Terrance.

Maria covered her mouth and her black eyes sparkled.

"It talks. It's a pet. Yours? Oh, you naughty girl."

"Shhh, don't tell anyone," Mandy said in Spanish. "My daddy would shoot it if he knew."

"Yes, yes, he would," Maria agreed, nodding so hard her black curls bounced.

111

"Aha!" thought Mandy. "Have you ever shot crows?" she asked in Spanish.

"Me?" Maria shook her head violently. "Only my husband can pick up the gun. That's the rule of his house."

"Gee whiz, do you obey all his rules?"

"Oh, yes, yes," she said.

"Would you shoot a gun if my dad told you to?"

"I would not touch a gun. It's a rule." She glanced at the ring on her finger and turned it casually.

"Would Teresa?"

"No, no. We follow the rules of the family." She looked away.

Maria stuffed the plastic into a bushel basket and walked toward the house.

"What would you do to me if I were your daughter and had a pet crow?" Mandy asked.

"You would *not* have a pet crow if you were my daughter."

"I wouldn't?"

"No. You would not if your father hated crows."

"But I'm learning a lot," Mandy mused, half to Maria, half to herself. "Having a crow makes me think."

"Think? Women do not need to think. We are told what to do."

Mandy followed Maria, stroking Nina's feathers and thinking about what Maria had just said. "Do you believe women should be told what to do?" she finally asked.

"No," Maria whispered softly.

"Perfect! Ha, ha, ha," yelled Nina Terrance suddenly. Maria gasped.

"That bird!" she screamed. "She heard. She'll tell." She ran to the gate. "She'll tell my husband."

"No! No! She won't," called Mandy, running after her. "She just mimics. It doesn't *mean* anything."

Maria's terror triggered a mixed-up reaction in Nina Terrance, and she flew down the strawberry field above her, screaming, "Ha, ha, ha. Very funny. Ha, ha, ha."

Barbara was coming out of the greenhouse, where she had been spreading seeds to dry. Maria opened the gate and rushed to her, wringing her hands.

"The bird will tell. The bird will tell my husband. I shot the gun. Your husband asked me."

"Maria, dear," soothed Barbara, putting her arm around the trembling young woman. "What *is* the matter?"

Maria was so upset now that even Barbara could not understand her Spanish, and so she led her into the family room and sat her down in the rocker. When she was calmed Barbara sat down beside her.

"You must not be afraid of your husband," said Barbara in Spanish. "I have wanted to speak with you for a long time about the money you earn. My husband and I each put our own earnings in our own personal checking and savings accounts for the future. I manage my earnings for the house. He manages his for the farm."

"I know there is a better way," Maria finally said. "I do want to change the family rule. Can it be done without pain?"

"I think so," said Barbara. "Bring your husband over here someday soon and we'll talk; I hope we can plan a better arrangement for you both."

Maria was smiling and talking when Mandy came in the door and made herself a cheese sandwich. When a break in the chatter came, she gathered her courage and walked over to her.

"Maria," she said in Spanish, "what did you shoot with Daddy's gun?"

"A raccoon," she answered.

"Crows?"

"No, no. I could not hit a crow. Too smart. It was a raccoon. He said I could. I lied to you. I asked him. He did not order me. They're good eating."

Mandy sat in silence.

11
Permission

Nina Terrance walked in the window Sunday morning.

"Cak-ca," she said and waited until Mandy had dressed, then hopped down the steps behind her. Barbara was talking on the bedroom telephone when Mandy opened the door.

"I don't know anything about it," she said and hung up.

"Who was that?" asked Mandy.

"Some theatrical agent, a woman who said she wanted to know if that talking crow on TV was yours. If so, she wants to sign you up for a Miami appearance. What's this about a crow on TV?"

"Nina Terrance slid down the slide and led Barney around at the shopping mall yesterday. Eyewitness News televised her. But how did she know to call here? I didn't give my name."

"Her daughter recognized you. Apparently you said the crow could talk."

Mandy sat down on the bed. The refrigerator door snapped open and she sprinted into the kitchen as Nina Terrance tossed a string bean out of the vegetable box, which she had also opened.

"Hey," Mandy shouted. "Get out of there." Nina flipped out the lettuce and a tomato and was reaching for the butter when Barbara came running in.

"This is too much," she said, looking at the mess on the floor. "It is really time for that crow to depart."

Grabbing Nina around the wings and body, Mandy ran to the door with her and threw her out.

"RRrrack," Nina protested and flew to the woman's-tongue tree, where she sulked and moaned.

The phone rang again. Barbara answered, frowned, and said she knew nothing at all about the crow. The next time it rang she did not move to answer it.

"Let's get out of here," she said to Mandy. "This is going to go on all day." She went to her room for her car keys and purse. The phone rang on and on and finally, unable to stand it any longer, she picked it up.

"Oh, Fred, it's you!" she exclaimed happily. "No, I wasn't busy exactly, just slow."

"Did what?" She rolled her eyes and looked at Mandy. Putting her hand over the receiver, she whispered, "Dad thought he saw you on TV . . . with a crow."

"Uh-oh, here it comes," said Mandy, biting her lips together.

"Well, she's right here," said Barbara, and held out the

phone. "Your dad wants to talk to you."

Slowly Mandy reached out for the instrument, her mind playing games. "I will. I won't. I will. I won't."

"Hello?" she said in a small voice, then raised her eyes to the ceiling as she listened. "You think you saw me on TV in the shopping center . . . with a talking crow?" Mandy's mouth felt full of cotton balls. "Barney? You saw Barney?" She shifted her weight from her left foot to her right and back again.

"Do I have a pet crow?" The moment was upon her. Mandy lifted her eyes to meet her mother's. Barbara's face was expressionless, showing neither encouragement nor disapproval of the lie Mandy felt was going to come out of her mouth. Then something overwhelmed her.

"Yes," she answered, so softly Barbara could barely hear her. "But she will soon fly off with the other young crows."

Mandy said no more, but Barbara could hear her husband's voice vibrating the receiver and she felt sorry for her daughter.

"I what?" Mandy gasped. Barbara turned her back and planned a quick death for Nina Terrance. "The vet," she thought, "the vet would make it easier."

"I can keep her? I can? It's okay? Oh, Daddy."

Barbara spun around on her heel and stared at Mandy.

"Oh, Daddy, I love you so. Nina Terrance, that's the name of the crow, is so funny, you'll like her. She eats cheese and eggs and cake; but never never wild strawberries or bananas." She held the phone close to her ear while her father talked.

"Mommy was right. She said you might not mind my

117

having a crow; but I was scared to ask you." She looked at her mother and smiled openly. "Daddy, hurry home. Nina Terrance puts money in her own bank in the gumbo-limbo tree and . . ." She stopped talking as Jack came to the phone.

"Do I want to write the lead story for *The Waterway Times* about my crow? I don't think so; I'm too busy keeping her out of trouble."

Mandy laughed and talked briefly to Carver, and then Drummer got on the phone.

"Drummer, I miss you. I'll be so glad to see you. You'll love this funny crow."

She was describing her antics, but Drummer had clicked off.

"Mommy," she said jumping around in circles, "he says I can have her. He says I can keep Nina Terrance."

"I am not so sure this is wise," said Barbara. "After all, your father does not know the circumstances of her early life. Maybe you and I should think this over."

"Perfect!" screamed Nina Terrance from the back step.

Mandy turned and looked at her mother.

12
Enemies

Nina Terrance did not knock on Mandy's window the next morning, and Mandy immediately began to worry. She poked her head out to find her crow. The woman's-tongue tree was making rustling sounds in the breeze and the bees were gathering on the hibiscus flowers, but Nina Terrance was nowhere to be seen. After dressing, Mandy hurried downstairs to find Barbara stirring a pot of grits.

"Nina Terrance has been very useful," Barbara said as Mandy leaned over the pot to smell the sweet cereal.

"How's that?"

"Maria called last night. The crow scared her to her senses. She told her husband about shooting the gun at the raccoon and he just laughed, so she told him she wanted to manage her money for the house and children. He agreed!

He had been talking to friends, too. A Puerto Rican at the bank is going to help them."

"That's wonderful," exclaimed Mandy. "It really is. And as far as I'm concerned that's a front-page story." Mandy slipped to the refrigerator and sneaked a piece of cheese while her mother spooned out the grits. "And now I *know* I can recognize a front-page story when I see it."

"I'm sorry our time alone is almost over," Barbara said.

"Me, too," replied Mandy, picking up her bowl.

"I thought since this was our last night together, we should go out to dinner—get all dressed up. Would you like that?"

"Oh, yes." Mandy spun around and stared at her mother. The Tressels never went out to eat. "Can I wear my new blue dress?"

"Yes, indeed," replied Barbara. "I thought we would go to the Old Bedford Inn, the one with the waterwheel and the old-fashioned fireplace."

"That's as fancy as a jasmine tree in full bloom," said Mandy. "My social studies teacher told me they serve roast beef and Yorkshire pudding there."

When Barbara had departed for work, Mandy ran to her room to make sure that her dress was not wrinkled. She took out her socks to see if they needed to be bleached, then polished her black sandals. Satisfied that her clothes were just right, she jumped down the steps and ran outside. She had almost forgotten that Nina Terrance had not come calling this morning.

When she could not find her in Piney Woods, Mandy

walked into Waterway Village and knocked on Mrs. Howard's door.

"She was here at dawn," she said. "She took a spoon from the sandbox and hid it in the tree. But I haven't seen her since.

"By the way, I just talked to Mr. Hathaway. He said he had been answering the telephone almost constantly . . . calls for Barney."

"Do people call Barney? Do they like *him*, a crow chaser?"

"Well, some do and some don't," said Mrs. Howard, catching a glimpse of her spoon in the tree. "Some want to cast the dog in bronze. Others want him locked up." She poked the spoon with her cane.

"How did they know who Barney was?"

"Didn't you see the show? The reporter couldn't find you, so he interviewed Mr. Hathaway. Al was so pleased, he claimed that Barney was the answer to all crow problems. He claimed he could 'lead those thieving birds' like the Pied Piper of Hamelin led rats out of the country." She poked once more and the spoon fell to her feet.

"Did he say that?"

"Yep. You missed a good show." Picking up her utensil, she put it in her apron pocket and limped back to her apartment.

"When Drummer comes home," she said, "tell him to climb up this tree for me. That crow has my fork and tea strainer up there."

"I'll get them for you," said Mandy. She stepped into one

of the twisted air roots of the fig, then to another, threw down the utensils, and climbed down. Mrs. Howard smiled.

"When are your menfolks coming home?" she asked.

"Tomorrow. And I'll be glad to see them, even old rejection-slip-editor Jack."

Mandy walked out over the golf course searching the trees for Nina Terrance. Suspecting she might be at the shopping mall, she hopped aboard the village bus and rode into the parking lot. There sat Nina Terrance on top of the slide. Her crop was full of food and Pete Moore was coaxing her to eat more.

"Make her talk! Make her talk!" a boy shouted to the hardware store owner.

"Shoot her," said an elderly gentleman in baggy slacks who was approaching the crow.

"Why, for heaven's sake?" Mandy asked him.

"They steal little birds' eggs, and I like little birds."

"But they chase hawks and owls that also eat little birds, and they clean up the dead animals on the highways."

"If I had my way I'd poison that bird."

"They eat mice and insects of all sorts," Mandy answered. "Would you really do that?"

"I've done it many times before. I'm an old farmer from Iowa. Crows are pests. Mark my word. Let this bird come to the shopping mall and get fed and a hundred will follow. This place will be a pit for disease."

Nina Terrance was strutting on the top of the slide and Mandy, exasperated by the conversation with the man, darted to rescue her bird before someone killed her.

"Cak-ca," she called from the foot of the slide and held

up her hand for Nina to alight on it. "Let's go home. Some people here would like to poison you."

"Ha, ha, ha. Very funny. Ha, ha, ha," screamed Nina Terrance, then flew to a woman who had flashed a quarter. She took it, circled her head, and came back to Mandy's hand. Mandy closed her fingers on Nina and clutched her to her chest.

"Hey, what are you doing?" said Pete Moore. "That's my crow." He took Mandy's arm and held it.

"She's nobody's crow. She's free."

Pete pulled Mandy toward him as he reached out to take the crow from her.

"Ca! Ca! Ca! Ca!" Mandy pinched her nose, rattled out the sound, and released Nina Terrance. She flapped across the parking lot and disappeared in the direction of Waterway Village.

"Come back," shouted Pete. Then he turned upon Mandy.

"You scared her away." He was angry, but suddenly his mood changed. "You're right. She *is* free. I'm going to catch her and put her in a cage. I want to keep this crowd coming to my store."

Mandy wrenched herself away from Pete Moore's grip and, darting around the cars, ran the five blocks to school. The bell was ringing as she slipped into her seat and covered her face with her hands. Nina Terrance was in trouble. Her life had been threatened twice in one morning.

School dragged slowly by, and when the three-o'clock bell rang Mandy was the first one out of the building. She ran home through Piney Woods searching and watching for Nina, who was nowhere to be seen.

When her mother got home from work Mandy was dressed and sitting rigidly on the straight-back chair in her room waiting for her.

"What's wrong?" Barbara asked. "You look pale as a moonflower."

"It's Nina Terrance. I've got to keep her away from the shopping center now."

"What now?"

"One man threatened to poison her, and Pete Moore is going to catch her and put her in a cage."

"Good thing Daddy's coming home."

"It really is. He'll help me."

Barbara pulled on a red dress with white cuffs and collar, then looked at herself in the mirror. This was indeed a special occasion, Mandy thought. Her mother had on a brand-new dress.

"Let's go out the front door like ladies," said Mandy and, moving gracefully on her heeled sandals, led the way. The hours of practice were paying off.

The dining room was lit with candles and smelled of pine and flowers. Barbara ordered the roast beef dinner for them both, and although Mandy smiled, she could not raise her spirits to the occasion. The man with the baggy pants loomed before her, poison in hand, and Pete Moore seemed to chuckle in her daydream as he slammed the door on a trap.

By the time the mince pie came, Mandy was so unhappy she could not wait for the dinner to be over. Barbara seemed to share her gloom.

"Let's get out of here," Barbara said. "I'm worried about that crazy crow." At home she tucked Mandy into bed, reassuring her that all would be well when her father came home.

Early the next morning, to Mandy's great relief, Nina Terrance knocked on the window. Mandy leaped from her bed and, throwing up the screen, took her into her arms.

"You're going back to the sable palm, and stay there until I come for you," she said. "And I am going to stuff you so full you will sleep all day."

As she approached the tree, Kray gave the harass-the-owl call from a limb almost directly above Nina and Mandy. Nina Terrance struggled at the sound and clawed the air.

Kray saw the struggling young crow.

"Caaaw," he called seven times, then added, "Wha, wha, ah." This was the rescue-the-crow call. Over the Glades came the crows of Trumpet Hammock, beating their wings hard in response to the summons. They alighted above Mandy and caaawed furiously at the crow who lived with people.

Their voices touched off ancient emotions in Nina Terrance and she bit Mandy's hand. With a cry Mandy released her, and Nina fell, caught herself on her wings, and flew to a low limb.

"Cak-ca," Mandy called, trying to get her back. Before Nina could relax, Kray had dropped to her side. The young bird stared at him, blinking and lifting her head feathers in concern. The crows in the trees above caaawed without letup. Kray hopped to another branch. Nina Terrance hopped to his side. The crows synchronized their caaaws into one voice, intense and full of conviction. "Come away with us."

Kray flew to a more distant twig. Nina followed. Mandy ran a few steps toward them. The leader of Trumpet Hammock was leading Nina Terrance away.

"It's all right!" Mandy called. "Daddy won't shoot you. Come back. Come back."

At the edge of the woods Nina Terrance hesitated. Kray scolded her, the crows caaawed on; then a guard bird announced the owl, and as one, the birds departed to harass the enemy.

Nina Terrance sat alone in a tall pine at the edge of the saw grass prairie. Mandy ran to her calling cak-cas of affection. Nina stared after the crows, and although Mandy coaxed her down with her gentlest sounds, she sat as if transfixed. An hour passed, the sun shone obliquely through the limbs announcing the lateness of the hour, and Mandy started home.

"I think the time has come," she said to herself. "Nina now knows she is a crow."

Flinging open the gate, she stopped still. Nina Terrance was knocking on the door.

"Come in," Barbara called. Mandy slid into her chair and plopped her elbows on the table. Happily she watched Nina Terrance walk the floor like a queen.

"I wish Daddy was home right now. People want to poison and cage Nina Terrance and this morning the crows almost lured her away. I want Daddy to see her before something happens. Can I leave her in the house today?"

"Not on your life. She'll have everything tossed out of the refrigerator and more vases broken."

As if she understood Mandy's intentions, Nina Terrance walked to the door. Barbara let her out and she flew to the woman's-tongue tree. As she disappeared among the leaves, Mandy had a strange feeling. Something in the way Nina Terrance moved made her feel she would not see her again. She ran to the door.

"Cak-ca," she called. Nina answered but did not appear.

When school was over Mandy took the bus to the shopping mall to check on Nina Terrance. She was grateful to learn she had not been there all day, and although Pete Moore blamed her for scaring the bird to death with her funny noises, she did not care.

Hurrying through Waterway Village and across the golf course, she began calling to Nina. After a long search she found her in the saw grass walking toward Trumpet Hammock. Her wings were drooped and the feathers on her throat were pulsating.

"What's the matter, Nina?" Mandy asked, picking her up. "You look so sad."

"Cak-ca."

Mandy returned her to the sable palm and went home for food for the crow, wondering if her father would ever meet the improbable Nina Terrance.

When, much later, she and Barbara were sitting before the TV set, Mandy arose, still troubled, and slipped her arms around her mother's neck. "I've had a strange day with Nina Terrance," she said. "She's sad. Do you think she knows the hunters are coming home?"

"Heavens, no. She's smart, but that's going too far."

"All the crows were sad today," Mandy went on.

"Maybe one of their own was killed."

"I don't think so. I think they know Daddy and Carver and Jack are coming home."

"That's ridiculous. What makes you think that?"

"You and I are different, now that the menfolks are coming home. We're not as cozy anymore."

Barbara looked up at her daughter. "You're right," she said. "We're not. I'm not as relaxed. My mind is already on the routines and schedules. . . . Maybe the crows do know."

13
The Villain

Mandy was asleep when her father and brothers returned. The front door slammed open and awoke her. The floors shook and Drummer ran up the steps two at a time.

"Look what I got youv!"

"What did you say?"

He held up the blue-and-green scarf as Mandy switched on the light. "The scarf," he said. "I found it." He wrapped it playfully around her head.

"Drummer," Mandy said to herself. "No. But . . . of course. Drummer says 'youv' when he's excited." She shook her head and slowly unwound the scarf from her head. "It's more beautiful than I imagined," she said, holding it up in the light. "Thanks a whole lot, Drummer. Thanks." Her voice was almost inaudible.

"I missed you," he said. "But I sure had a good time."

"I missed you," said Mandy in a low voice.

"How long have you had that pet crow?"

"Ever since I told you about my friend Nina Terrance."

"I see. That figures," he said thoughtfully and got to his feet. Mandy slipped on her house shoes, thrust her arms in her dressing gown, and started toward the stairs.

"You sure fooled me," he said. "I really thought she was a person."

"I had to keep her a secret even from you. You want to be a hunter."

"I sure do," he said, puffing up his small straight chest, but Mandy paid no attention to him. She was halfway downstairs. With a leap she rushed into her father's arms.

"And where is this famous crow?" he asked. "You sure pulled a good one on me, raising a crow and teaching it to talk, all right under my nose; me the most ferocious crow hunter of Dade County."

He held her at arms' length and smiled wryly.

"Was she a secret from everyone?"

"Except Mom."

"That figures. You two are thick as lovebugs. That mommy of yours sure spoils you."

"I would have told *you*, but I thought you would kill her."

"I might have at that! But I doubt it. Course I can't very well bop her off now. She's a celebrity." He shook his head. "We were having dinner in a restaurant when she came on the screen. I recognized Barney right away and laughed 'til my sides hurt when that crow yelled, 'Here comes that damn dog again,' and ran Barney almost dead."

"How did you teach her that?" asked Carver with a grin of admiration.

"Jack taught her somehow. She imitates his voice." They laughed and Jack shrugged his shoulders, disclaiming all responsibility.

"Here we have a page-one heroine in our midst," said Jack, "and I didn't even believe it."

"Well, now *you* can write the story," said Mandy. "You'll meet her tomorrow."

"Aw, no. This is your assignment. You know all about her. How about it?"

"No, sir," she said and slid from her father's arms.

"Well, tell us about the trip," said Barbara, and everyone began talking at once. When Mandy dozed in the chair, Barbara urged her to bed.

"I'll set a place for Nina Terrance at the breakfast table," she promised her sleepy daughter, "and tomorrow you can show off *your* adventure."

"Maybe she won't appear," said Mandy at the foot of the steps. "She knows that Jack and Carver and Daddy shoot crows."

"Tell her she's invited," said Jack.

"I don't think it will help," she said and walked up the steps.

Curled in her bed, she listened to the doors banging again and the shower raging. Deep voices echoed in the hall and she decided that these were good sounds after all.

The crickets were fiddling away on their wings with their hind feet when Mandy awoke. It was very late for her. She stumbled to the window and looked for Nina Terrance. The yard, field, and woods were quiet; the blue earring shone in the crotch of the woman's-tongue tree.

"Cak-ca," Mandy called. A breeze clattered the pods, but no crow came to her call.

Mandy hurried downstairs to find that breakfast was almost over. Her father tapped one of the two unused plates.

"Where's Nina Terrance?" he asked.

"I don't think she will come to our house anymore. She's seen every one of you with a gun."

"Not Drummer," he said. "Why don't you and Drummer go get her and bring her here. We'll feed her until she comes to like us. Go on, Drummer, help Mandy."

"I'm too tired," he said, slumping down in his chair and fairly falling asleep on his plate.

"I'll go," said Mandy and ran outside.

Nina Terrance was not in the gumbo-limbo tree or under the leaves of the sable palm. She was, however, in the pine tree where the crows had lured her the other day.

"Cak-ca," she called to Mandy, then took to her wings and soared out over the saw grass, alighting in a clump of spider lilies shining like white stars near the footbridge log.

Mandy waded out into the water that covered the feet of the saw grass now that the rainy season had returned. She hurried toward Nina Terrance.

An explosion like the slamming of a car door sounded near the spider lilies and Mandy jumped back in terror, knowing full well it was Old Monster's jaws closing on prey. No longer confined to the moat with the rising of the water, he was now hunting all across the Everglades. Regaining her composure, she walked warily back, then stopped still fifty feet short of the huge reptile. Crow feathers hung from his mouth.

"No," she cried. "Nina, where are you?"

"Nevah, nevah, nevah," called Kray in distress as he came back from the saw grass where he had been hunting frogs. He had spotted the black feathers hanging from the mouth of the alligator.

"Kaa, wha, wha, ah," he mourned and flew like a shadow into the trees.

"Cak-ca," called Mandy.

Giving Old Monster a wide berth, she crossed the log and crouched low as she entered the hammock. She would not believe the dead crow was Nina.

"Cak-ca. Nina."

Above her head the crows hunched in the shadows waiting for Kray to give the "All's well" caw and release them from their fears.

Presently he sounded it and the crows went about their routines again. Mandy struggled through the tall strap ferns and crawled over a moss-covered log. Suddenly Nina alighted on her head, and she reached up and took her eagerly in her hands. Hugging her close, she ran home through the twigs and grasses tearing at her.

Near the strawberry field Nina struggled to be free. Mandy clutched her closer and was tucking her under her shirt, when Nina reached out and pecked her belly so hard she cried and dropped her. Nina flew into the gumbo-limbo tree.

"Come on," Mandy hollered. "Daddy won't hurt you. He says I can keep you around the house."

The crow just lowered her head and cawed morosely, then pecked her toe as if to change the subject. Mandy walked into Piney Woods and sat down. Instantly, Nina flew to her shoulder. Reaching into her pocket Mandy pulled out a cookie and gave Nina one bite.

"Come with me," she urged. "I want you to meet Daddy." Mandy reached for her. Nina jumped away. She reached again. The crow floated off and alighted on the ground. Mandy got to her knees and threw herself forward. The crow moved lightly out of reach.

"Okay," she said. "You win. They'll have to come to you." Picking herself up off the ground, she brushed her clothes and went home.

"She won't let me catch her," she said as she came through the door. "She has seen you guys and won't come any farther than the gumbo-limbo tree. You'll have to do the walking."

"Hey," said Jack. "This is beginning to sound like a joke. Bird won't come to men. Men go to bird."

"You're going to have to convince her you like crows," said Barbara. "And that's not easy to do."

"How do we do that?"

"Print Mandy's story about the fish Mrs. Howard let go," said Drummer.

"What's eating you, Drummer?" snapped Jack.

To avert an impending quarrel Fred sent Drummer to the front yard to pick up the morning paper. He jumped to his feet and fled the room.

While the men and Barbara were carrying the dishes off the table, Mandy wrapped some fish and potatoes in waxed paper and stuffed it in her pocket. Then she picked up her books and went out the door.

As she passed under Nina Terrance's money tree she heard her call and sat down. Presently Nina walked out from under a saw palmetto leaf. Mandy offered her the fish. Nina sat still eyeing it, then rushed in, grabbed it, and hopped out of Mandy's reach.

"Ha, ha, ha," screamed the bird.

"You're terrible, Nina," scolded Mandy. "You won't let me even touch you." She rocked back on her heels. "I know why. I'm a predator, not a friend. I'm trying to catch you for some evil purpose and you know it." She grinned at the bird and ran to tell her father.

He smiled and cocked his head. "She knows you're after her. Your attitude has changed. You've switched from a mother to an owl." He picked up his machete to trim the bananas. "To fool a crow you have to be the best actress in the world."

At the bus stop Mandy was greeted by a friend of Drummer's.

"Hey, Mandy," he said, "can you bring the crow to school?"

"I can't make her do anything," answered Mandy. "She'll come if she feels like it. She's free."

Mandy pushed to a seat and sat down. Ellen Percy, the class president, beat another girl to the empty seat beside Mandy.

"Mom says you can come visit today," she said.

"I have to feed my crow."

"Can I help?" she asked eagerly. "I raised a baby robin once."

Mandy smiled and invited her to come to the woods with her.

"Thanks," said Ellen. "Mary and Chris and Tom were coming to my house. Can they come too?" Mandy nodded.

"I sure want to meet that crow," said Ellen, sliding closer. "She's keen."

At three o'clock twelve kids paraded down the school steps behind Mandy and filed across the recreation field to the school bus. They climbed aboard, and after a brief fight for the seat next to Mandy, Ellen won the position again.

"Will Nina Terrance talk for us?" she asked.

"Only if she feels like it. I can't make her talk. She has to be scared or see something that she associates with the moment she learned the words."

"Neat," said Ellen.

A perspiring gang of excited young people followed Mandy up her driveway, around the greenhouse, and down the path by the fallow strawberry field. Maria and Teresa were rolling up the last of the plastic ground cover while casting an eye out for the crow.

Mandy called to them as she led her troop of friends into Piney Woods. Stepping over the white hatpin flowers by the path, she stopped under the gumbo-limbo tree. Two jerking leaves told Mandy that Nina was up in the limbs.

"Cak-ca," she called softly.

"Cak-ca," the bird replied, stepped from the shadows, and studied Mandy's intentions. She sensed she would not try to catch her and flew down to a low limb.

"Hi." Mandy held up the food she had packed this morning. Feeling that the children were also friendly, Nina Terrance flew down to Mandy and pecked the food. The kids crowded in.

"Ha, ha, ha. Very funny. Ha, ha, ha," said the crow. A small boy gasped in astonishment, a girl giggled, then the whole crowd broke into delighted laughter.

"Here comes that damn dog again. Who said that? On the path. Okay. Perfect." Nina Terrance, as if inspired by the children, reeled off her entire English vocabulary. Tom laughed, Chris doubled over, and Ellen stood still, her mouth wide open.

Nina Terrance glanced toward the Glades. "I got youv," she screamed, leaped onto her open wings, and dodging twigs and limbs, sped toward Trumpet Hammock.

"Hey, Drummer's here," said Chris, looking around. "Hey, Drum, where are you?"

"Drummer's not here," said Mandy.

"I thought I heard him."

"What did he say?"

"I got you."

"That was Nina Terrance, the crow."

"Funny, she sounded just like Drummer."

Mandy bit her lips together and led the troop back toward the house as Drummer came running down the path from the Glades.

"Hey, Drummer *is* here," said Chris and ran to meet him. Drummer pushed past his friend and got in front of Mandy. His face was pale, his eyes wide.

"Did you see Nina Terrance?" Mandy asked. "She flew in your direction."

"No." He wiped the perspiration from his face with his

arm and wedged into the crowd of kids.

"Your crow is just super," said Ellen as she caught up with Mandy at the gate. "She's almost uncanny."

"She's smarter than my teacher," said a small redheaded girl whom no one had particularly noticed. The kids laughed, talked, and tossing pine cones into the air, tramped into the yard.

Then they saw Jack and Carver leaning over the engine of the SAAB. Like a wave they rolled up against the car and peered in.

"Looks like rings this time," said Jack, straightening up to behold Mandy's friends.

"Man, a SAAB," said Tom, patting the fender. "This is one of the best cars in the world. You put oil in the gasoline tank, right?"

"Right, a fifty-nine." Jack opened the door and showed Tom the mahogany trim and leather upholstery. The red-headed girl dropped to her hands and knees and peered up under the rear of the car.

"The early morning dew," she said, standing and wiping her hands against each other. "Plays hell with mufflers. Yours is about shot."

Grinning, Carver got down on all fours. "She's right," he said to Jack and laughed.

"Get out the typewriter, Jack," said Drummer. "Time for a *Waterway Times.*"

"And do we have news this time!" Jack slapped Mandy across the back.

14
The Deed

In the feathery light before dawn, Mandy lay awake in her bed, staring at the ceiling. She heard her father walking below; then the water pump started up and she knew he was in the shower. She traced him from the bathroom to the kitchen to his desk, mentally watched him opening the account book and picking up his pen. She counted slowly now to give him time to complete his work. The strange hoot of the great blue heron barked out from the Glades, and simultaneously she heard her father's footsteps cross the living room to the kitchen, going out the back door and down the steps. The screen door slammed.

Mandy flung her legs out of bed, grabbed her shorts and a checkered shirt off the chair, put them on, and picking up her sneakers, stole barefooted to the steps and down to her mother's room.

She placed her hand on the doorknob but did not turn it. She stared at the wood grain in the panel of the door, her thoughts in conflict. Finally she turned around and walked back upstairs.

Lightly she rapped on Drummer's door, heard no response, waited, and finally stuck her head in. He was rolled up in the sheets asleep. Mandy glanced about the room, her eyes skimming from the drawing board topped with coffee cans bristling with pens and brushes to his clothes and books on the floor. She tiptoed to him.

"Drummer?" she called softly. "Wake up."

His dark lashes fluttered as if he were coming from some distant place he was reluctant to leave.

"Drummer." She shook him again. He rolled into a ball and mumbled a few obscure words. "Drummer," she insisted. He opened his eyes and looked bewilderedly into hers, then pushed on his elbows and propped himself up.

"What do you want?"

"Drummer, I've got to talk to you."

He slowly sat up, blinking out of his fog of sleep.

"Is something wrong?" He cowered and Mandy realized she must look like a mountain lion looming over him. She pulled up a chair and sat down.

"Drummer, have you been using the shotgun?"

"Me? I wouldn't do that."

"Tell me, please tell me. You may be in danger of getting hurt." Drummer was now wide-awake.

"I didn't." His eyes turned away from hers.

Mandy twisted her fingers.

"That's good, because if you did, I'll have to get rid of Nina Terrance."

"Why?" Throwing off the sheet, he crossed his legs. His toes curled tightly under.

"Because whoever shot her parents is in for it. That person is going to be pecked and chased as if he were an owl. Nina Terrance is imprinted on him. He has become her enemy. She can't help it."

"You mean she can recognize one person from another?" Drummer asked nervously.

"Yes. Think back real hard, Drummer. When you shot up the nest, what did you say?"

"I don't know."

"Well, Nina Terrance does."

"She does?"

"She talks, you know, and one of the things that she says is 'I got youv.'"

"Sounds like Daddy or Jack or Carver. They shoot crows all the time."

"But she imitates your voice, Drummer. It's you. You always say 'youv' when you're excited, not 'you.'"

He did not answer.

"Did you shoot them?"

"Well—" He took a long breath and moved closer to Mandy. "Yes. It's terrible being eleven, almost twelve, in this family. I can't do anything. Can't hunt. Can't drive. Can't . . .

"Mandy, what'll I do? I'm scared. She does know me. She dives for my face, like yesterday in the woods. She was after me."

Mandy touched his hand. "Oh, Drummer. That's horrible. You've got to stay out of the woods."

"Will that work?"

"I think so. She never comes into the yard when you guys are around. I'll never feed her again. Mommy was right. She'd be gone now, far, far away, if I hadn't been so selfish and dumb." Mandy rubbed the perspiring palms of her hands on her shorts. "If she hurts you, I'll never forgive myself. Honest . . . it's awful." She smiled grimly at her little brother.

"You like her, don't you?"

"She's the most exciting thing in the world. She's better than a friend."

"Better than me, too, huh?"

"No. Never. Not better than you, Drummer."

"Please don't tell about the gun, Mandy."

"But you're going to get hurt. Daddy knows a lot about crows. He knows what you should do. He could even break the imprint of you in her mind, I'll bet. Then I could keep her."

"Please, Mandy, please don't tell."

"Daddy's really not mean at all, Drummer. Don't be afraid of him. Just talk to him. Look at me. I thought he'd punish me and kill my crow if he knew about it, so I didn't tell him. Now I wish I had. Nina wouldn't be chasing you. He'll understand about the gun, too."

"You're a girl. That's different."

"No, no it isn't." Mandy walked to the window and looked out, staring down on the coconut palm, wondering what to say to Drummer now.

"Drummer, I'm going to talk to Mommy. She'll help us."

"Please, no. Don't," begged Drummer. "I'll keep to the road and yard. She'll go back to the crows soon."

Mandy pressed her head against the sill. "But she won't disperse," she said softly. "She won't go far away like the other young crows. It's too late. I've held her back from her natural behavior by feeding her through her dispersal time. I wanted to keep her so badly."

"I *am* scared," said Drummer, crossing the floor to her. "She goes for my eyes."

"Oh, no!" Mandy spun around and clutched Drummer's shoulders and looked into his wide scared eyes; then she turned and ran back to her room. Opening the screen, she leaned far out her window. Piney Woods where Nina slept was fresh and glittering from the night's rain. The mockingbird was on his singing post. The owl hooted his return from the hunt.

Mandy knew what she had to do.

Half an hour later as she came down the stairs for breakfast, she found Jack and Carver at work on *The Waterway Times.*

"You won't write the story," said Jack, looking up, "so I interviewed the residents."

"Man, do we have stories about Nina Terrance," said Carver. "Benny said she read a paper over his shoulder." He laughed. "And Pete Moore claims she can open the cash register."

"Thanks for the page-one story of the year," Jack said, but Mandy did not hear him. She was thoughtfully packing her lunch box. Only one sandwich lay on the bottom.

All day at school the kids sought out Mandy again to question her about Nina Terrance and invite her to play with them. She answered automatically, like a cassette tape, for she was concentrating on Drummer's problem. She saw his face everywhere—in the math book, on her English paper, in the Spanish book. And he had no eyes.

"Mommy," she cried to herself at the end of the day, when she was finally opening her locker before going home. "I need to talk to you so much. You make things better. But this time you can't."

As she boarded the school bus a boy announced that Nina Terrance was going down the slide at the hardware store again, and they all shouted to the bus driver to stop at the mall.

Drummer climbed into the bus. He shoved through the standing kids and sat down beside Mandy. He was very pale and he looked frightened. Mandy slipped her arm around him.

"Stay on the road when you get off the bus," she said. "I'll keep her at the mall until you get home."

As she stepped off the bus at the shopping mall she looked back. Drummer was huddled against the window.

Hardly had she taken three steps before Nina Terrance came winging across the parking lot, braked her wings above Mandy's head, and dropped to her shoulder. Nina glanced up at the bus, saw Drummer, and flattened her feathers in fright.

"I got youv!" she said, and Mandy felt her heart sink into her stomach.

"It's true. Cak-ca."

Nina did not answer. She was studying the sky and wind.

"Ca! Ca! Ca! Ca!" she screamed, using the alarm signal of the crows for the first time, and took off, flapping hard in the direction of Piney Woods.

"Hey, she's gone," Ellen exclaimed.

"Aw, nuts," said Tom.

"Who's for a swim?" called the grandson of a Waterway Village resident. "Get your suits and we'll meet at the pool."

Mandy ran away from the crowd of kids and hurried across Waterway Village to Piney Woods. Near the sable palm she heard the throaty comments of an angry crow and glanced up to see Nina Terrance stealing through the limbs, head down, eyes focused, as she stalked toward the road and the school bus. Mandy chased her, shouting at her, but she had no food in her pocket, no crusts in her lunch box.

A scream sounded out.

"Drummer!" Mandy gasped and, running full speed, darted over logs and around the cutting blades of the saw palmettos. She found Drummer near the road, bent over, screaming in pain.

"Let me see. Let me see."

"It hurts."

Mandy pulled his hands away from his eye and looked into it. It was watering badly, but no blood flowed. She wiped his face with the tail of her shirt and he blinked and opened his eyes.

"I'm blind," he said, tears pouring out of his eyes.

"Oh, no. Drummer, no." She threw her arms around him and rocked him to her chest. Presently he stopped crying and his quaking body calmed. He pulled away from her, blinked, and opened his eyes.

"I'm okay." He rolled his eyes.

"Can you see?"

"Yes." Turning his head, he looked at her and smiled in relief. "I can see."

Mandy slowly got to her feet and, taking her little brother's hand, led him toward the house while watching the trees for Nina. When they reached the back steps, Mandy glanced back at Trumpet Hammock. It was ominously silent, floating like a misty ship on its sea of grass. She pulled Drummer inside and slammed the door.

"Come here," she said.

"What are you going to do?"

Jack and Carver were not yet home, and her father was in the banana grove. Her mother was still at work.

Mandy walked to the gun rack and picked up the shotgun. She turned to Drummer.

"Where do you put the bullet?"

"NO! Mandy, NO! I'm not going to show you."

"Yes, Drummer . . . you will or I'll tell."

"Mandy." A sob welled up from his chest. "You can't do that."

"Drummer. Show me what to do."

His icy fingers touched Mandy's hand as he pushed a lever and broke open the shotgun. He reached into the ammunition box, took out two shells, and placed one in each barrel. Then he cracked the gun closed.

"When you're ready to shoot, push this button." He pointed. "It's the safety. To aim, sight down the barrel and put this bead on the target. Squeeze slowly." His voice broke.

"Go upstairs," she said. "When we are asked about Nina Terrance, we say that the crows came and took her. They do that, you know."

Mandy held the gun awkwardly at her side as she went out the door and down the path. She would have to be swift. Nina Terrance knew all about people with guns.

At first she searched the gumbo-limbo tree. Nina was not there. She walked on, crawled under the dead leaves of the sable palm, and sidled down the corridor to the reading room. Nina Terrance was on the ground playing with her earring. Mandy raised the gun, aimed, and fired.

A shower of black feathers spewed up in the smoke and the fire.

"Ca! Ca! Ca! Ca!" yelled Kray.

"Kaa, wha, wha, ah." Nina Terrance cried the dying crow call to tell all the crows of her fate.

Mandy backed out of the palm room and ran all the way home sobbing uncontrollably. Inside the family room she placed the gun in the rack, turned, and ran upstairs.

She threw herself across her bed and cried until she was exhausted.

The door opened and Drummer came in. He crossed the room and lay down on the bed beside her.

"Nevah, nevah," mourned the crows of Trumpet Hammock. "Nevah, nevah."

"Oh, Drummer, why did you kill those beautiful, beautiful birds?" Mandy's breath involuntarily sucked in. Drummer did not answer.

Two crows flapped out across the Everglades, flying toward some new land deep in the interior. Three more followed them, crying and mourning.

"Say it," said Mandy. "Say it like we must."

"How?"

"The crows of Trumpet Hammock came down in the yard today and took Nina Terrance."

"No," Drummer sobbed.

"Nevah, nevah," moaned three more crows and, bowing their wings deeply, flew over the shimmering Glades to find the other crows. One of these was Kray.

"Yes, Drummer. You must. Now say it."

"The crows of Trumpet Hammock came down in the yard today and took Nina Terrance."

Mandy slipped her arm around him and he curled his knees under him like a rabbit.

"Nevah." Three more crows flew a wide circle around the Tressel house and winged their way to the pines in the Miami suburbs. "Nevah, nevah."

"She was your friend," Drummer said.

"It's okay." Mandy wiped her tears with the bedspread.

"I killed her," said Drummer.

"We both killed her. I wouldn't let her disperse. I kept feeding her even when Mommy told me not to. I ruined her. She would have flown away and never hurt you if I hadn't been so selfish and cruel."

The back door opened and Mandy heard her mother come in. She called to see if anyone was home, then went to her room.

"Aren't you going to Mom?" Drummer asked. "You always do."

"No."

Mandy stood up and stepped softly to her mirror and closed her eyes. Quietly Drummer put his feet on the floor and shuffled hesitatingly to the door. He opened it and walked downstairs to find his brothers.

After a long time Mandy opened her eyes. She could hear the mockingbird singing, the trade winds rattling the woman's-tongue tree. From below, her mother's footsteps clicked across the kitchen floor. Mandy started to go to her, then stopped.

"Time to flap my own wings," she said and picked up her red notebook. Slowly turning her head she looked out through the sunny window.

"It's scary," she whispered. "But gee, how far I can see."